MW01031112

THE GUNSMITH

479

Steel Disaster

Books by J.R. Roberts
(Robert J. Randisi)

The Gunsmith series

Gunsmith Giant series

Lady Gunsmith series

Angel Eyes series

Tracker series

Mountain Jack Pike series

COMING SOON!
The Gunsmith
480 – The Friendly Mine

For more information
visit: www.SpeakingVolumes.us

THE GUNSMITH

479

Steel Disaster

J. R. Roberts

SPEAKING VOLUMES, LLC
NAPLES, FLORIDA
2022

Steel Disaster

ISBN 978-1-64540-814-7

Chapter One

Clint heard a long scream.

He immediately knew it wasn't a human. It sounded more like steel-on-steel, which he occasionally heard when he was either riding in a train or was near a train.

But rather than the sound of a train breaking to stop at a station, this went on longer, and then, suddenly, he heard the blood curdling sound of steel crashing.

His first thought was that the sound was to his east, so he whirled his Tobiano in that direction and rode hard. The crashing sound went on too long, and he knew he was about to see something horrifying. When the sound finally stopped it was replaced by other screams, and this time they *were* human. As he got closer-and-closer, he saw clouds of smoke from the locomotive's steam engine. A mix of voices began calling for help, others calling out orders.

When he crested a rise and was able to get a good view, he saw what he was afraid he would see.

A tangled mess of iron, some from tracks that had been bent, but most of it from the train cars that had apparently collided and had been throw from the tracks.

As he rode down toward the carnage he was able to figure out what had occurred. A section of track had apparently been bent and broken. The engineer had probably braked too late, and when the locomotive came to the twisted section it jumped the track, causing the cars behind it to collide with each other. The result was the derailing of the majority of the cars. The only one still on the track was the caboose.

As he reached the chaos, people were still running from the caboose, while others seemed to be crawling from the derailed passenger cars. Cows and horses had jumped from the derailed stick cars, which had jumped track but remained upright. Unfortunately, the same was not true of the two passenger cars, which were laying on their side, as was the locomotive.

As Clint dismounted, he saw men and women, some more bloodied than others, desperate to escape from the cars, some stumbling, others crawling. He wanted to help, but who needed help the most? Where should he begin?

He decided to start with the locomotive. The engineer and fireman might need help getting away from the engine which, even lying on its side, was still belching smoke. Clint feared an explosion might be imminent.

As he ran toward the locomotive he yelled to people, "Get away! Get as far away as you can!"

Some people heeded his warning, others stared with wide, glazed eyes, as they stumbled.

"Help these people!" he shouted, pointing to the staggering ones. "Help them get away."

Suddenly, he spotted the conductor. His hat was gone, and he was bleeding from a gash on his head, but he recognized him from his uniform.

"The engineer," the man shouted to him, pointing, "he must still be in there."

"Get these other people back," Clint said, stopping in front of the man. "I'll see what I can do."

The conductor immediately turned and began barking orders to the fleeing passengers.

Clint reached the overturned locomotive and tried to see through the smoke. He heard someone coughing, then saw a man crawl from the wreckage. He grabbed the man beneath the arms and dragged him to safety.

"Are you the engineer?" he asked.

"N-no." The man coughed. "I'm the fireman. The engineer's still in there."

"What's his name?"

"Buster, his name's Buster."

"Lie here and catch your breath," Clint instructed, and ran toward the locomotive again.

He peered through the smoke as it stung his eyes, but couldn't see if anyone else was trying to crawl free.

"Buster!" he shouted. "Buster!"

When there was no reply, he felt he had no other choice. He reached the engine and started to climb aboard. The metal was hot, but he tried to ignore the pain it was causing to his hands.

When he reached the top, he was able to look down into the locomotive. He immediately saw a man lying on his back, recognized him from the grey clothing as the engineer.

"Buster?" he called.

The man didn't move. Clint was about to drop down into the locomotive when he saw that the man's eyes were wide open but staring at nothing. Blood had soaked into his uniform and leaked from his head. The man was quite dead.

As smoke engulfed and blinded him, he saw no point in risking his life any further. There was still the possibility of an explosion. So he turned and leaped from the twisted engine . . .

Chapter Two

As he hit the ground he rolled in an attempt to avoid injuring his legs. When he stopped rolling, he got to his feet and tried to clear his tearful eyes. He felt someone grab him beneath the arms and drag him away from the smoke. When they stopped, he realized it was the conductor.

"Buster?" the man asked.

Clint shook his head.

"He's dead. The fireman?"

"He's over here," the conductor said, leading the way.

When they reached the fireman, he was sitting up looking around. They joined him and saw people still crawling free of the wreckage.

"There are more people inside," the conductor said. "We have to help them."

"It looks like we're going to need more help," Clint said, coughing to clear his burning throat. "Like a doctor. Was there one on board?"

"Maybe as a passenger, but I don't know," the conductor said.

"What's the closest town?" Clint asked.

"The next stop is Dexter," the man said.

"How far?"

"About five miles."

"Would there be a doctor there?" Clint asked.

"It's a big enough town," the conductor said.

"I can ride there for a doctor, and more help," Clint offered.

"We need you here," the man said. "You might be the only able-bodied man."

Clint looked around.

"I'll find somebody who can ride and put them on my horse," he said.

"That sounds good," the fireman said.

"What are your names?" Clint asked.

"I'm Willy," the conductor said, "he's Lester."

"Can you both move?"

"I can," Willy said. "Lester?"

The man bent his arms and legs.

"Looks like I can," he said.

"Okay," Clint said. "Let me find a rider. You two assess the damage, and see which people need the most help."

"Right!" Willy said.

Clint got to his feet and moved toward the largest group of people. Some of them were coughing, others bleeding, some lying or sitting on the ground, others standing. He picked out the fittest looking young man.

"Can you ride?"

"Yessir," the man said.

"There's a town about five miles up the track," Clint said. "Take my horse and ride for help. We need men, and we need a doctor. Got it?"

"Yessir, I got it."

"There's my horse," Clint said, pointing to his Tobiano. He would rather have given the man a horse from the stock car, but the ones that had escaped the carnage had run off, getting as far away as possible.

"Go!" Clint shouted.

The man ran toward the Tobiano, mounted up and rode.

Clint turned toward the others.

"There are still people on board who need help," he shouted. "Anybody able enough, follow me."

He ran toward the derailed passenger cars, followed by three or four men. They reached the point where Willy and Lester were standing.

"Still people on board?" Clint asked.

"Sounds like women and children," Willy said.

"We have to get them off," Clint said to all assembled.

Several men moved toward the overturned cars accompanied by Lester.

"There are probably people on the caboose," Willy said. "It didn't derail, but it stopped abruptly enough to injure passengers."

"Let's take a look," Clint said.

He and the conductor ran to the caboose and climbed aboard. They heard people banging on the doors, and realized they were jammed shut at each end.

"I'll try this one, you try the other," Clint said.

"Right."

Clint climbed on the end of the caboose and tried the door. It was jammed tight.

"Help! Help!" a voice came from inside. It sounded like a woman.

"The door is jammed," he called back. "How many of you are there?"

"We're in here with a group of children," she said. "We're two teachers."

"Can you get out the windows?" he asked.

"Some of the children are hurt," she called back. "But I can drop some of them out a window."

"All right," Clint said, "let's start with that. You drop them and I'll catch them."

"A-all right."

"But hurry," Clint said, "the engine might explode any—"

A loud explosion cut him off, and the caboose jerked forward, dislodging him and throwing him to the ground . . .

Chapter Three

Clint hit the ground hard, and the air was knocked out of him. The exploding furnace in the locomotive had jarred the entire length of the train. People screamed.

He got to his feet and saw that the conductor had also been jarred loose. He ran to the man.

"Are you all right?"

"Just tryin' to catch my breath," the man said.

"Yeah, me, too. What about your door?"

"Jammed."

"Did you talk to anyone?"

"No, but I could hear some crying from inside."

"There are a couple of teachers in there, with students," Clint said. "They're going to drop some of the kids from a window."

"They'll get hurt."

"I'll catch them," Clint said. "Meanwhile, find something we can use to pry the door open."

"Like a crowbar?"

"Like a length of iron," Clint said. "Part of a track."

"Ah, good idea!" the man cried, and ran.

Clint turned and ran back to the end of the caboose. He saw a woman looking out a window.

"I thought you'd gone," she said.

"I'm here," Clint said. "Let's go."

"I'll drop some of the little ones first."

"I'm ready."

She withdrew her head, then a small child appeared, dangling from her hands.

"Okay, let go!" he shouted.

She did. The child screamed, and then she was in Clint's arms, staring up at him.

"You're fine," he said, putting her down. "Just wait here, all right?"

"Yes, sir."

Clint looked up, and another child came dangling out the window. When he caught the boy, he was a little heavier. He put him down next to the girl. For the next few minutes, he caught child after child, heavier than the one before. Eventually he noticed that it took two teachers to hang the children out the window, as they got larger.

Finally, the first teacher stuck her head out the window.'

"That's all," she said. "The others are too big, and we have a few who are hurt. What about the door?"

"We're working on that."

When Clint turned to look at the assembled children, he saw a middle-aged woman approaching them. She looked harried, but lucid.

"Do you need help?" she asked. "With these children?"

"Yes, please. Take them to a safe distance."

"Of course." She grabbed two of them by the hands. "Come along, Kids."

"Where's Miss Rafferty?" one girl asked.

The woman looked at Clint.

"Must be their teacher," Clint said. "She's still inside. We're getting her out."

"She'll be fine," the woman said to the child. "This nice man is going to help her."

Several of the children stared behind them at Clint as the woman led them away.

The conductor came running over awkward carrying a length of track.

"That'll do," Clint said. "Come on."

He climbed up on the back of the caboose, and the conductor handed up the length of track. Clint reached down and pulled the man up, which wasn't easy.

"All right," Clint said. "Let's try."

"The door opens inward," the conductor said.

"Miss Rafferty!" Clint called. Stand back from the door!"

"All right!" she called back.

First Clint and Willy tried to use the three-foot length of track as a battering ram. The door didn't budge.

"Let's try and pry it loose," Clint said.

"Use the other end," Willy said. "It's sharper."

They reversed the track and Clint found he was able to slide the sharp end between the door and door jamb.

"This might work," he said. "Let's try it."

They leaned on the rail, and, for a moment, nothing happened, but then, abruptly, the door slammed open. They tossed the rail away and entered the caboose.

"Miss Rafferty?" Clint said.

The woman who stared at him was young and pretty, with long blonde hair.

"Yes," she said, "I'm the teacher. This is Miss Long."

Miss long was older and rather plain looking.

"Thank you so much," Miss Long said.

Clint saw several children who had been injured. The teachers had tried to bandage their injuries.

"Let's get you all out of here," he said.

"It's all right, children," Miss Rafferty said. "We're getting out now, thanks to this nice man."

"Clint," he said. "My name's Clint."

Chapter Four

Willy climbed down and Clint handed him the injured children first, and then the teachers.

"Where are the other children?" Miss Rafferty asked.

"They're over there," Clint said, and pointed "A lady came by and took them.

"I see them," she said. She was about five-and-a-half feet tall and looked up at him. "I'm Delores. Thank you so much, Clint." She stood on her toes and kissed his grimy cheek. "Thank you."

She carried one child, while Willy carried two more, and Miss Long led another couple by the hand. They joined the rest of the children at the top of a hill.

As Willy came back, Lester ran over.

"We're havin' some trouble," he said.

"Lead the way," Clint said.

He and Willy followed the fireman to one of the overturned cars.

"There are some injured people in here, but we can't get to them."

Clint climbed atop the overturned car and looked in a window. Several people seemed to be pinned between seats.

"We were gettin' them out, but when the furnace exploded it shifted the car, and they got trapped."

"We don't have enough men?" Clint asked.

"Not nearly."

"I sent somebody to town for help," Clint said. "Can they wait?"

"I doubt there's gonna be another explosion, but a couple of them are bleedin'," Lester said.

Clint looked around, saw a shattered window.

"Lower me down, and I'll see what I can do."

Lester took one hand, Willy the other, and they lowered him into the car. He felt the car shift beneath his weight, and realized it wasn't sitting solidly. It could have shifted again at any moment.

He made his way to a point where two people were pinned. One was a large man, the other a smaller woman in her fifties. Both were bleeding.

"I'm going to do what I can about your wound, and then we'll try to get you out."

"Okay," the man said.

"Oh please, hurry," the woman said.

Clint looked around for something to be used as bandages. He found several carpetbags, opened them and found some clothing inside. He tore strips of it, then went back to the people.

The woman was bleeding from the arm. Clint tied a bandage as well as he could, and managed to staunch the flow of blood, somewhat.

He moved to the man, who seemed to have a puncture wound he couldn't see.

"Where are you bleeding from?" Clint asked.

"I think it's my left side," the man said. "It was hurting for a while, but now it feels numb."

"Let me see if I can get a look."

Clint tried to get beneath the seat that had the man pinned. He was right. A piece of glass seemed to have pierced the man's side. Clint thought he could reach it, but if he pulled it out, the bleeding would increase.

"I see it," Clint said, and explained the situation. "We have a doctor on the way from town. Just try to hang on."

"I-I'll try," the man said, but Clint could see he was fading. He had that cloudy look in his eyes that Clint had seen before on men just before they bled out.

He thought he might be able to stuff some makeshift bandages around the wound, but if he touched that piece of glass he might dislodge it, and then the bleeding would increase.

"I'll be back with the doc," he told them, hoping he was telling the truth.

***

When he climbed back out from the passenger car, he stood for a moment and surveyed the area from atop the car. He could see that many of the passengers were either sitting or lying down. The ones who were lying were also covered with blankets he assumed had been recovered from the stock cars.

He dropped back to the ground where Willy and Lester were waiting.

"How they doin'?" Lester asked.

"I managed to stop the bleeding on the woman," Clint said, "but I'm afraid the man's going to bleed out if we don't get a doctor here soon."

At that point they heard the sound of approaching hoof beats. A buggy came into view, moving fast, with a single man in the seat. They went to meet him as he reined his horse in.

"I'm Doctor Hendricks," the man said, climbing down and then retrieving his bag. "Looks like you need me."

"There are plenty of injured, Doc, but we need you for one in particular. This way."

The doctor was a tall, rangy man in his fifties who moved quite easily as he followed Clint and the railroad men.

"There are two passengers trapped in this car, and both are bleeding," Clint said. "The man particularly needs you."

"Then let's get in there," Doc Hendricks said.

Clint lowered the doctor into the car first, telling him where the man was injured.

"Are there more men coming from town?" Clint asked the man.

"They were gatherin' as many as they could," the doctor said.

"Are you a doctor?" the woman asked.

"I am, Ma'am."

"Thank God!" she breathed. "My arm hurts—"

"In a minute, Ma'am," he told her. "I have to see to this gentleman."

Clint watched as the doctor moved toward the man. He watched as the sawbones examined the man, then picked up his bag and moved to the woman.

"Doc?" Clint asked. "How is he?"

Hendricks looked up at Clint and said, "I'm afraid he's dead. He lost too much blood." He then moved to the woman.

Clint rubbed his face with both hands and said, "Goddamnit!"

Chapter Five

Clint, Willy and Lester walked the length of the train, to see if any other passengers were still trapped. While they were doing that, they heard several wagons approaching. In moments two buckboards loaded with men appeared.

Clint grabbed several men and brought them to the passenger car where the woman was still trapped. The doctor had stopped the bleeding, but it was going to take a few of the men to free her from the seat that was pinning her.

"Be careful moving around in there," Clint said. "The car isn't sitting solidly."

"When you get her out, put her on one of those buckboards. I'll check on the other injured people and see who needs to get back to town first," the doctor said.

"Is there somebody there who can treat them?" Clint asked.

"I have a nurse," Hendricks said, "but once I've examined all these folks, I'll head back. The ones who aren't injured can wait for a ride back to town."

"Sounds good," Clint said. "Thanks, Doc."

"Sure thing."

"Oh, one thing. The young man who rode into town on my horse."

"He's fine," Clint said. "Just a bit exhausted."

"And my horse?"

"The horse seemed fine," Doc said. "Not even winded. We had him taken to the livery. The fella there knows his horses. He'll care for your animal."

"Thank you, Doctor."

The doctor went to examine the rest of the passengers.

Clint got together with Willy and Lester. They were passing a canteen back and forth, and when Clint joined them, they passed it to him.

"Thanks." Clint took a sip, then realized it wasn't water, but whiskey. "Whoo!"

The railroad men laughed for the first time since the crash.

"That's Doc's," Willy said. "He said it would be good medicine."

"Shouldn't you fellas head to town?" Clint asked.

"We represent the railroad," Willy said. "We should stay til all the passengers are seen to. Then we can get Buster out of there, so he can be buried."

"What's left of him," Lester pointed out. "That explosion pretty much took him apart."

They turned when another mounted man arrived from town. Clint saw the glint of his badge as he dismounted.

"I'm Sheriff Gaze," the man said. He was in his forties, a dour look on his face "What the hell happened here?"

"We'll show you," Willy said.

He and Clint walked the lawman to the front of the wreckage.

"There," Willy said. "Somebody pried up about twenty feet of track. When the locomotive hit it, that was it."

"You mean this was deliberate?" the sheriff asked.

"A case of sabotage, sheriff," Clint said.

"Why didn't the engineer stop?" the lawman asked.

"He didn't see it in time," Willy said. "Somebody just removed the rails. There was nothing for him to see."

"Sonofabitch!" the sheriff said. "How many hurt?"

"A couple of dozen," Willy said.

"Including children."

The sheriff turned as one buckboard loaded with injured headed back to town.

"You two work for the railroad?" the sheriff asked, looking at Willy and Lester."

"I'm the conductor," Willy said.

"I'm the fireman," Lester said.

"And you?" the sheriff asked, turning to Clint.

"I was riding by and heard the commotion. When I came to see what happened, I saw all this."

"And stayed to help?"

"Yep," Clint said. "I put a man on my horse and sent him to town for help."

"And you don't know anythin' about this?"

"Nope," Clint said. "Like I said, I was just passing by."

"On your way to where?" the sheriff asked.

"Nowhere in particular," Clint said. "I didn't know about your town."

"Have you ridden through this part of Texas before?"

"Well, sure," Clint said, "but I haven't stopped in every town."

"Why are you questioning him, Sheriff?" Willy asked. "He's the reason a lot of these people are alive."

Clint didn't think that was true, but he appreciated the conductor standing up for him.

"I'm just askin' questions to try and find out what happened," the sheriff said. He looked at Clint again. "What's your name?"

"Clint Adams."

The lawman and the railroad employees all stared at him.

"The Gunsmith?" the sheriff asked.

"Yes, sir."

The lawman looked at him, hesitated a moment, then said. “Let’s talk again when we get back to town.”

“Whatever you say, Sheriff,” Clint replied.

Chapter Six

But they didn't get back to town for some time.

Willy wanted to make sure everyone had been removed from the train—including the deceased.

Along with the dead engineer, several passengers had also been killed. Willy, as the conductor representing the railroad, felt responsible.

At last satisfied himself that everyone—living, injured and dead—had been claimed from the wreckage, Willy was ready to leave.

Clint's horse had been brought to him from town, as well as a mount for Willy.

"It was decent of you to stay with me, Clint," Willy said, as they mounted up."

"It didn't seem right to leave you alone," Clint said. "After all, you did hit your head in the crash, and for all I know, you could pass out at any minute."

"I honestly felt like it a few times," Willy said.

"Well, let's get back to town and Doc Hendricks can take a look at you."

"I've got to get a telegram off to the home office," Willy said.

"You can do that first thing in the morning," Clint said.

"They're gonna want to send somebody out to investigate."

"That's fine," Clint said. "That's expected. The sheriff is going to want to talk about this some more. After you see the doctor, you can rest and deal with all of this tomorrow."

"I've never been through anything like this before," Willy said. "All these people, hurt and killed . . . those children . . . our engineer . . ."

"I know," Clint said, "it's a terrible thing."

Willy fell silent after that and they rode the rest of the way quietly, which suited Clint . . .

***

Upon arriving in town, Clint left Willy at the doctor's and took the horses to the livery. From there he stopped at the sheriff's office. The man looked up from his desk as Clint entered the office.

"You're back," the lawman said.

"Yes," Clint said. "The conductor is with the doctor. He's going to send a telegraph to his home office in the morning. They'll probably send an investigator out."

"Good," Gaze said. "I don't mind tellin' you I don't know what to do here."

Clint sat down.

"I've never seen anything like this before," he said. "All that wreckage . . . it was a lucky thing there weren't more dead."

"I'm just glad none of those kids were hurt," the sheriff said. "I'll find out in the morning just how many people were killed. Oh, hey, you want a drink?"

He didn't wait for an answer. He took a bottle and two mugs from his bottom drawer, poured and handed one to Clint. He downed it and set the mug on the desk.

"I need to get myself a hotel room and get some sleep," Clint said, standing.

"I'll need to talk to you and the railroad men in the mornin'."

"I'll bring him here," Clint said, "after I get a good breakfast into him. He feels responsible for this whole thing."

"What? Why? He's not at fault."

"He represents the railroad," Clint said. "He's the kind of man who feels things deeply."

"Well," Gaze said, "someone will have to convince him he's not at fault. The railroad's not at fault. It's whoever tore up those tracks who's responsible."

"Hopefully," Clint said, "he'll come to realize that."

Clint headed for the door.

"I have to ask you somethin'," Gaze said.

"What?"

"You weren't headed here, were you?"

"I told you, I never even heard of Dexter."

"So you're not . . . looking for someone."

"No," Clint said, "and I'm not looking for trouble."

"That's good."

"I'll see you in the morning," Clint said, and left the office.

Chapter Seven

Dexter was a good sized town that had several hotels and boarding houses. They all made room for the injured and displaced passengers, with promises made to the owners that the railroad would cover all costs.

Clint found Willy housed in the same hotel that he was and knocked on his door the next morning. When the man answered the door, he was fully dressed.

"Ready for some breakfast?" Clint asked.

"I've got to send a telegram."

"After breakfast," Clint said. "You need to eat."

The conductor nodded, stepped out into the hall and closed the door.

"Did you sleep?" Clint asked, as they went down to the lobby.

"Surprisingly, yes," the man said. "I think I was asleep even before my head hit the pillow."

"That's good. Any dreams?"

"No," the man said, "it was a black, dreamless sleep."

The hotel lobby also had tables, some occupied by people eating, some not.

"This is as good a place as any to eat," Clint said. "Let's sit there."

He steered the conductor to a table against the wall, with only two chairs.

They ordered their breakfasts and drank coffee while they waited.

"The sheriff wants to see us this morning," Clint said.

"I need to send my telegram."

"We can do that first," Clint said. "No problem."

The waiter brought their breakfast.

"Let's eat," Clint said.

***

Clint waited outside the telegraph office for Willy. When the man came out he seemed different, more relaxed.

As they walked to the sheriff's office Willy said, "I didn't think I'd have that much of an appetite."

"It's only natural," Clint said. "After a horrible experience like that, you've got to do something normal, like eating breakfast."

"I guess so."

"Did you get an instant reply to your telegram?" Clint asked.

"Yes," Willy said. "They're sending an investigator right away. I'm to stay here and wait."

"Will the railroad be covering all expenses?" Clint asked. "I mean, for the passengers."

"Oh yes," Willy said. "They'd rather do that than get sued."

When they reached the sheriff's office Willy stopped.

"What do I tell him?" he asked Clint.

"The truth," Clint said. "You didn't do anything wrong."

Willy nodded, and then entered the office.

Sheriff Gaze was standing off to one side, leafing through some wanted posters.

"Looking for me?" Clint asked.

"No," Gaze said. "I check the posters every so often, just to keep up."

He put them down, walked to his desk and sat.

"Have a seat," he invited.

Clint and Willy both sat.

"You're the conductor," the lawman said. "What's your full name?"

"William Herman."

"And how long have you been with the railroad?"

"I've been employed by various railroads for over twenty-five years. I'm currently employed by The Texas Panhandle Railroad Company."

"How long has this railroad been in existence?"

"It's very new," Willy said. "It's been running for about four years, now."

"Where does it run?"

"Through twenty-six counties of the panhandle from Oklahoma to New Mexico."

"It's a passenger line?

"It has passenger and stock care," Willy said.

"Tell me about the engineer," Sheriff Gaze said.

"Buster Posey is—was—a very experienced engineer with over forty years experience."

"Forty years?" Gaze said. "How old was he?"

"Buster . . . was in his seventies."

"Isn't that a little old to be operating a train?" the lawman asked.

"Buster came out of retirement for this job."

"I see."

"Why all the questions, Sheriff?" Clint asked. "The railroad is sending out their own investigator."

"This happened in my patch, Mr. Adams," Gaze said. "I'll look into it until I'm relieved by a railroad man."

That made sense to Clint, if the sheriff was possessive about his "patch."

Chapter Eight

The sheriff continued to question Willy, and finally moved on to Clint. The questions were much the same as before, trying to determine what The Gunsmith was doing in the Dexter area. Clint's answers didn't change. He had never heard of Dexter and was just riding by when he heard the train crash.

"I guess that's it for now," Sheriff Gaze said. "When will the railroad's investigator be getting here?"

"According to the telegram," Willy said, "he's already on the way. Should be here in a day or two."

"So what should we be doing in the meantime?" Gaze asked.

"The railroad will pay all expenses for boarding passengers, whether they're injured or not," Willy assured him. "In the meantime, the railroad would like someone to keep an eye on the wreckage until their investigator can have a look at it."

"I'll put a deputy on it," Sheriff Gaze said, "but I've only got one."

"I can take a shift," Clint offered.

"I appreciate that," Gaze said. "Between you, me and my deputy, we should have it covered."

"The railroad will appreciate that, Sheriff," Willy said. "They really want to find out who was behind this mess."

"And what if it was just an accident?" the lawman asked.

"It wasn't," Clint said. "Somebody actually removed that stretch of track, knowing that the engineer would never see it in time."

"Well," the sheriff said, "I'll be real interested to see what your investigator comes up with."

"I'm sure our man will be happy to work with you, Sheriff," Willy said.

"I'll appreciate it," Gaze said.

"I'll go out and take a shift until your deputy relieves me," Clint said.

"I'll get him out there in about four hours," Gaze offered.

Clint and Willy left the office and walked toward the livery for Clint to saddle his horse.

"Any idea who the railroad is sending?" Clint asked.

"No," Willy said, "I won't know until he gets here."

"Well, I'll ride out for my shift on the wreckage."

"I suppose I should've volunteered, as well," Willy said.

"I think it's better for you to remain in town," Clint said. "After all, you represent the railroad. Some of the passengers may have questions only you can answer."

"I suppose that makes sense."

Willy watched Clint saddle the Tobiano and walk him out of the livery.

"I'll be back in about four hours," Clint said, as he mounted up. "Let's get a steak together."

"Suits me," Willy said. "I really appreciate everything you've done, and will do, Clint."

"I couldn't very well just ride by when I saw what happened," Clint told him.

"A lot of men would have," Willy said.

"Then they wouldn't be men."

***

When Clint reached the crash site, he tied the Tobiano to a tree, then walked the length of the wreckage. When he reached the caboose, he was about to turn back when he heard something. He stopped and listened. It soon became obvious someone was in the caboose.

It was most likely someone stealing what they could carry. He leaned back against the caboose and waited for them to come out. There was two of them. They started to climb down awkwardly, their arms filled with booty.

When the first one made it down, he saw Clint standing there.

"Hey," he said, "this is our stuff."

"What's goin' on?" the other one asked.

"There's another man here," the one on the ground said, "I'm tellin' him this is our turf."

"No," Clint said, "it's not. All of this belongs to the railroad."

"What do you care?"

The man was armed. Clint assumed the man he couldn't see was also armed.

"I'm here to make sure no one takes anything," Clint said.

The second man dropped down, carrying a gunny sack that was obviously loaded.

"How do you plan to do that?" the second man asked, dropping the sack.

The items the first man was holding also hit the ground.

"There's two of us, and one of you," he said. "If I was you, I'd look the other way."

"I can't do that," Clint said. "If one of you goes for his gun, I'll kill you both."

The first man laughed.

"You tryin' to scare us?"

"I'm trying to save you," Clint said.

The man laughed again.

"You think you're Wild Bill Hickok or somethin'?"

"No," Clint said, "not Wild Bill, although he was a friend of mine. My name's Clint Adams."

The second man caught his breath.

The first man said, "You expect us to believe you're the Gunsmith?"

"What you believe is up to you," Clint said. "Whether you live or die is also up to you."

They stared at him a moment, then the two of them just walked away, leaving their booty behind.

Chapter Nine

Clint kept walking the length of the wreckage, checking to see if the looters came back, or if others tried. He was fairly sure the wreckage was clear when he heard a horse approaching.

He didn't know what Sheriff Gaze's deputy looked like, but he did know his name. When the rider came into view, he saw that it was a young man.

"Mr. Adams?" he asked, swinging down from his horse.

"That's right."

"I'm Deputy Banner," the young man said. "Ted Banner."

That was the name, but this could still have been another looter. But the young man was wearing a badge, and Clint decided not to be paranoid.

"You can go back to town now," the deputy said. "I'll be relieved in four hours."

"I caught two men trying to loot the caboose and drove them off. I don't think they'll be coming back."

"I'll keep an eye out," the deputy promised.

"Okay," Clint said, mounting up. "I'll see you back in town. I'll buy you a drink."

"Suits me."

Clint headed back to town.

***

Upon arrival in Dexter, he saw to his Tobiano, then went to the hotel. Since his shift at the train wreckage ended at 2 p.m. it was between lunch and dinner. But he was hungry, so he went to Willy's room and knocked on the door.

"You're back," Willy said.

"And hungry," Clint said. "How do you feel about an early steak?"

"I feel fine about it," the conductor said.

"Let's find someplace other than the hotel dining room."

"Suits me."

They left the hotel and walked until they came to a place called The Sunflower Café.

"This looks as good as any," Clint said, and they entered.

The first thing Clint saw was the sheriff, sitting at a table alone. The man looked up from his plate, saw them and waved them over.

"Join me," Gaze said, "You've found the best place in town for a steak."

"That's good to hear," Clint said. "I'm starving."

"Me, too," Willy said, and they sat.

The sheriff waved to a waiter and told him to bring two more steak dinners. Clint and Willy had coffee while they waited.

"How was it out there?" the sheriff asked.

"Quiet," Clint said, "sad. I caught a couple of looters."

"Did you kill them?"

"I let them go. There was no point in killing them. I dissuaded them, and maybe they'll do the same to others."

"Let's hope so."

The waiter came with their plates and they started eating.

***

They talked enough about Deputy Banner for Clint to be sure he had met the right man.

"I'm eating now because I'll relieve him at six."

"That makes me relievin' you at ten," Willy said.

"You don't have to—" the sheriff started.

"No," Willy said, "I think I should."

"Then I'll relieve you at two," Clint said.

"That late?" Willy said. "I thought I'd have the final shift."

"Looters might hit the wreckage that late," Sheriff Gaze said. "I'll have my deputy relieve Clint at six, and we'll start again. We'll keep an eye on everythin' until your investigator arrives. Do we know who it will be?"

"No," Willy said. "The telegram only said an investigator would be comin'."

"Hopefully it's somebody competent," Gaze said.

"We'll see," Clint said. "You were right about this steak. It's good."

"This is where I usually eat," the lawman said.

"Do you feed your prisoners from here?" Willy asked.

"Hell, no," Gaze said. "There's a café down the street from me. The food's awful, but good enough for prisoners."

Gaze pushed his plate away.

"Keep eatin'," he said. "I need to get back to my office." He stood. "There won't be a bill."

The sheriff turned and left the café.

"No bill?" Willy asked.

"Town's often feed their lawmen for free," Clint said.

"If that's true," Willy said, "how about some pie?"

"That sounds good to me."

"Think they have rhubarb?"

"Jesus," Clint said, "I hope not."

Chapter Ten

They went through another round of standing watch over the wreckage. When Clint came in from being relieved by Deputy Banner, Willy told him. "The investigator is here."

"Good," Clint said. "When is he going out there?"

"He wants to talk to us first," Willy said. "I arranged to meet him at the café at three."

"That's in fifteen minutes," Clint said. "We might as well walk over there."

"Let's go, then."

Willy came out of his room, and they walked down to the lobby.

"Who is it?" Clint asked as they left the building and headed for the café. "The investigator."

"Somebody you might know."

"What's his name?"

"He told me not to tell you."

"What?" Clint asked. "Why?"

"You'll see, I guess."

"Did you tell the sheriff we were meeting?" Clint asked.

"Yes, I did. But I don't know if he'll be there."

They reached the cafe and went inside. Clint didn't see any familiar faces. They sat at the same table as the last time they were there. Clint was able to keep his eye on the door.

"What can I get you gents?" the waiter asked.

"Just coffee for now," Clint said. "We're waiting for someone."

"Comin' up."

They drank coffee and waited. When a familiar face appeared, it was the sheriff.

"Not here yet?" he asked.

"No," Clint said. "Might as well have some coffee."

So the three of them drank coffee and waited.

"Who's the investigator?" Gaze asked.

"Willy's not saying," Clint said.

"Why not?"

"I guess I'll find out when he gets here."

A man appeared in the doorway, well dressed and groomed, wearing a bowler hat.

"Sonofabitch," Clint said, but his tone was good natured.

Both the sheriff and Willy looked at the doorway.

"Who's that?" the lawman asked.

"That," Clint said, "is Bat Masterson."

Both the lawman and Willy stared as the man approached with a big grin on his face.

***

Bat laughed his head off while he and Clint embraced. It had been a while since the two friends saw each other.

"What are you doing working for the railroad?"

"I was one of the very first railroad detectives way back," Bat said. "The owner of this railroad asked me to come here as a favor. I was nearby, so I agreed. Especially when I heard you were involved."

"Hardly involved," Clint said. "I was just riding by when it happened."

"Just what did happen?" Bat asked.

"Let's get some steaks and then we can talk," Clint said.

When they had their plates in front of them Clint allowed Willy to go first.

"I'll need to talk with the fireman, as well," Bat said, when the conductor finished.

"I'll take you to him after we're done here," Willy said.

"And what did you see?" Bat asked Clint.

"Just the aftermath," Clint said. "I heard the brakes, and the crash. It was all over by the time I got there."

"And what did you see after?"

"The tracks had been dislodged," Clint said. "The train derailed."

Bat looked at Willy.

"Two passenger cars?"

"Yes," Willy said, "and they weren't full, thank God."

"There were a couple of teachers with some students in the caboose," Willy said.

"Any of the children hurt?" Bat asked.

"Willy?" Clint said.

"I don't have a final number, yet," the conductor said.

"I'll talk to the doctor," Bat said. "The railroad wants to cover everyone's expenses, especially the injured ones."

"That's good," Sheriff Gaze said.

They finished their steaks and sat back.

"Who wants to take me out there?" Bat asked. "I should have a look."

"I'll come along," Willy said.

"Good," Bat said, "there'll be some questions you can answer."

They stood up and stepped outside.

"I'll stay here," the sheriff said. "My deputy's out there."

"I've got two more railroad men coming in tomorrow," Bat said. "They can sit on the wreckage for a while."

"That's good," Clint said. "I guess we'll see you later."

The sheriff went to his office while Clint walked with Bat and Willy to the livery stable.

Chapter Eleven

When they reached the crash site, Clint introduced the deputy to Bat Masterson. He could see the young man was impressed.

They walked Bat to the section of track that had been uprooted.

"This had to be done by more than one person," Bat said. "I don't see any hoof prints. Looks like they came out on a buckboard. Probably had to bring some tools."

He walked the length of the wreckage with Clint, Willy, and the deputy behind him.

"These cars, they're twisted," Bat said. "How fast were you going?"

"I'm not sure," Willy said. "Normal speed. Buster just had to jam on the brakes and when we hit that section . . ."

"Yeah," Bat said. "Let's get back to town so I can see the fireman."

"Right," Clint said.

Bat told the deputy he'd have some men out there the next day.

"The sheriff will be out later," Clint said.

Clint, Willy, and Bat mounted up and headed back to town.

***

They left their horses in the livery and walked over to talk to the fireman, Lester, who was staying in a rooming house.

"Lester, this is Bat Masterson," Willy said. "He's the railroad investigator."

"Masterson?" Lester said. "Glad to meet you."

"I just have a few questions," Bat said. "It has to do with what the engineer did just before the crash."

"Sure, go ahead."

Bat asked about the locomotive's speed, the engineer's reactions, Lester's reactions, who or what he saw just before the crash. Lester relayed all these thigs to Bat as honestly as he could.

"Okay, Lester," Bat said, "thanks."

"Can we leave town, now?" Lester asked.

"No, not yet," Bat said. "Not until my investigation is cleared. I'll let you know when that is."

"All right," Lester said. "Thanks."

Clint, Bat and Willy left the rooming house.

"I won't need you anymore today, Willy," Bat said, outside. "I want to talk with Clint."

"Okay," Willy said. "I'll be in my hotel room."

"I'll be sending a telegram to your home office to tell them I'm here," Bat said, "but feel free to do the same."

"Yes, sir."

Willy walked off towards his hotel.

"Clint, let's get a drink. What's a good saloon?"

"I haven't really had time to try them all."

"Then let's just go to the closest one," Bat suggested.

They found a saloon called The Oasis, a few blocks away and went inside. It seemed half full, and they were able to find a table that suited both of them.

"What do you plan on doing?" Clint asked Bat.

"Sticking my nose everywhere," Bat said. "There's a train depot here. I'll talk to the people there. Somebody must have had a reason for doing this."

"You'd think so."

"Nothing was stolen?" Bat asked.

"Apparently not."

"But why else would someone want to derail a train?" Bat asked.

"Sabotage," Clint offered. "Another railroad that wants this line?"

"Texas Panhandle is a pretty small, new railroad, Clint," Bat said. "I'm only working for them because the owner is a friend of mine. This kind of thing can drive them out of business."

"But it's not their fault."

"It doesn't really matter if it's their fault or not," Bat said. "This is a huge catastrophe for them. I don't know what I can find out that might be helpful, but I'm going to try."

"Well, I'll give you all the help I can."

"That's what I was hoping you'd say," Bat replied.

"I was hoping you'd say that," Bat said. "And I'm open to any suggestions."

"What do you have in mind?" Clint asked. "I mean, for a direction to go."

"I thought I'd talk to all the passengers," Bat said. "Maybe somebody was looking out the window and might have seen something."

"That sounds like a good start," Clint said. "But there were quite a few. I can help you, if we split them up."

"That's a good idea," Bat said. "It'll make things go much faster."

"Your friend must be anxious to find out the whole story," Clint said.

"He has a board of directors to deal with," Bat said, "and they want answers. That's what I'm here to find."

Chapter Twelve

In Amarillo, William Reynolds, the head of the Texas Panhandle Railroad Company, was sitting in a meeting with some of his board members.

"What do we know so far?" one of them asked.

"Just that the train derailed," Reynolds said.

"Was the equipment defective?"

"No," Reynolds said, "I heard from the conductor that someone tore up the tracks."

"Jesus! Why would they do that?"

"We don't know," Reynolds said. "Nothing was stolen. "So we're trying to figure that out. We sent an investigator to look into it."

"An investigator?" one man asked.

"Someone we can trust?"

"Yes," Reynolds said, "somebody I can definitely trust. Bat Masterson."

"Masterson?" one man blurted.

The man to that man's right put his hand on his arm.

"Masterson," the second man said. "That's good."

The other three board members agreed, and the meeting broke up.

"I'll let you know when I have some information."

They all nodded and left.

***

Outside the office, three of the board members went their own way. Two stood there with their heads together.

“Bat Masterson?” one of them said.

“That’s not a problem,” the first man said. “He won’t find anything.”

“How can you be sure?”

“We hired good men.”

“But Masterson,” the second man said. “The man’s a legend.”

“And he’s doing this because he’s friends with Reynolds,” the first man said. “He’s not a true investigator.”

“I hope you’re right,” the second man said. “We want this to happen fast.”

“Go home,” the first man said. “I’ll be in touch.”

“Right.”

The two men went their separate ways.

***

The next morning Bat and Clint split the names of the passengers between them and began questioning them.

"Why don't you take the teachers and the kids," Bat said. "I'm not very good with children. Besides, they know you already. You rescued them."

"Okay," Clint said. "I'll start with them."

The children and teachers were put into a boarding house. When he came to the front door and asked for them, Miss Rafferty came.

"It's all right, Miss Peabody," she told the woman who ran the boarding house, "this is the man who rescued us from the train."

"That's fine," Miss Peabody said, "but I still don't allow men upstairs in your room."

"I'm helping the railroad investigator with the accident," Clint told both women. "I can talk to the children down here, if it's all right with you."

"That's fine," Miss Peabody said. "I'll bring some tea out for you, and milk for the children."

"Thank you, Miss Peabody," Miss Rafferty said. "Come this way, Clint."

"I'd like to speak with you before the children come down," Clint said.

"All right," she said, sitting with her hands primly in her lap. "What can I tell you?"

"Anything you might have seen just before the crash," Clint said.

"What could I have seen?" she said. "We were in the caboose."

"Maybe you were looking out the window? Just before?" Clint suggested.

"I did look out the windows with the children," she said.

"But you didn't see anything?"

She shrugged.

"I was just answering the children's questions."

"About what?"

"About everything," she said. "Cows, horses, Indians, anything they could think of to ask. You know how children are."

"I don't," he said. "Not really."

"You're very good with them though," she said. "Just the short time you were with them, I could see that."

"I rescued them," he said. "Of course they'd like me."

"Do you want me to bring them down one at a time?"

"How many are there?" he asked.

"Here in the house, there are twenty," she said. "There are four still at the doctor's office."

"All right," Clint said, "why don't you bring down four at a time."

She stood up.

"Boys or girls."

"Let's mix them."

"All right," she said, and went upstairs.

Miss Peabody came out with tea, milk and cookies on a tray.

"These children are precious little things," the older women told him warningly.

"I understand."

She looked down her nose at him and said, "Have a cookie."

Chapter Thirteen

The first three groups of children talked eagerly with Clint. They were happy to see him, and the little girls giggled a lot. The boys were the ones who had stared out the train windows a lot, but the first three batches didn't see or hear anything helpful. Some said they saw horses and cows, but other than that, they had nothing to offer.

All the kids had cookies and milk, so Miss Peabody needed to bring refills.

"They're really so little," Miss Rafferty said, while they waited. "Even if they had seen something, they wouldn't know if it was important."

"They just have to tell me what they saw," Clint said. "I can decide if it's important."

"So you'll want to speak with Miss Long."

"Yes," Clint said, "but I'll take her last."

"You'll have to be gentle with her," Miss Rafferty said. "She's a little high strung."

"I'll keep that in mind."

"I'll get the next batch," she said, and went upstairs.

***

Clint talked with one boy who might have seen something. His name was Roy.

"Miss Rafferty," he said, "I'll keep Roy a minute. You can take the others back upstairs."

"Okay, kids," she said, "let's go."

"Aw, Roy gets to stay with Clint," one girl whined.

"Just for a minute," Miss Rafferty said.

When they had all gone up, Clint said, "Okay, Roy, tell me again what you saw."

"You mean the men?" the little boy asked. "I saw four men riding away from the train."

"Before it crashed, right?"

"Yes," Roy said, "I didn't see anything after the crash."

"Tell me about the men? Were they big? Small?"

"I couldn't tell," the boy said. "They were all on horses."

"Tell me about the horses."

"They were just horses. Big."

"What color?"

"Oh," Roy said. "Uh, two brown, one grey, and one had, oh, spots on it."

"A paint?"

"Is that what they call it?"

"Yes," Clint said, "a paint. Anything else."

"They rode up a hill."

"Did you see them get to the top?"

"No, sir."

"So you didn't see them look back?"

"No, sir."

As Miss Rafferty came back down the stairs Clint said. "Okay, Roy. Thank you." He looked at the teacher. "You can take him back upstairs."

"All right."

"And send Miss Long down."

"I will," she said. "Remember, she's high strung."

"I'll remember," he promised.

She went up with the boy and the other teacher came down the stairs slowly. She was smaller than Miss Rafferty, plain looking rather than pretty. She approached Clint keeping her eyes down.

"Sit down, Miss Long," he said. "This won't take long."

She sat, her hands in her lap.

"I just want to know if you saw anything. Maybe when you looked out the window."

"I—I didn't see anything," she said.

"Did you look out the window?"

"I suppose I must have, at some point," she said, "but I don't remember seeing anything."

"That's all right," Clint said, "it was a longshot that you might have spotted something. Thank you."

Miss Long went back upstairs and Miss Rafferty came back down. Miss Peabody also put in an appearance.

"Are you finished with the children?" the older woman asked.

"Yes, Miss Peabody," Miss Rafferty said. "They're back upstairs. You can clear the cookies and milk away. I'll walk Mr. Adams to the door."

Clint walked to the door with the pretty young teacher.

"I'm sorry we couldn't help you, Mr. Adams," she said.

"Oh, it wasn't a total loss," Clint said. "I think Roy might have given us something."

"Just remember," she said, "Roy is a very imaginative little boy."

"I'll keep that in mind, Miss Rafferty," Clint said at the door. "Good day."

"Good day, Mr. Adams."

There might have been a time when Clint could have asked the pretty young woman to dinner, but he was a little busy trying to help Bat with his investigation.

He walked down the steps and headed back to his hotel.

Chapter Fourteen

On the way to the hotel Clint came to The Oasis Saloon. He decided to go in for a beer and to just listen to some of the conversations. When he entered, the first thing he saw was Bat Masterson sitting at a poker table with four other men. Never let it be said business ever interfered with Bat's poker. Of course, he might have been there for the same reason Clint was, to listen to some of the conversations. Or, depending on who he was playing poker with, he could have been looking for specific information.

He knew Bat saw him, but his friend didn't acknowledge his arrival. He walked to the sparsely populated bar and asked the bartender for a beer.

"Comin' up," the man said.

He set the beer in front of Clint and moved on down the bar. Clint stood there, listening to all the talk around him, including what was being said at the poker table.

He was surprised to hear Bat telling the gents he was investigating the train crash for the railroad.

"It wasn't an accident?" one man asked.

"Not at all," Bat said. "Somebody pried up that track and caused the train to derail."

"Jesus," another man said, "why would anybody do that?"

"That's what I'm trying to find out," Bat said.

Two of the players looked like storekeepers, one a trail hand, and the fourth wore a suit, like Bat's. Obviously, he was a gambler.

"I thought poker was your business, Masterson," the gambler said.

"I have a lot of business dealings, Corbin," he said. "Sports, gambling, the law on occasion, literary pursuits. This I'm doing as a favor for a friend."

"Fifty. Do you have experience at this sort of thing?"

"As a matter of fact, I do," Bat said. "Call and raise fifty."

The game was obviously not big stakes, all the more indication that Bat was using the opportunity to glean information.

Clint sipped his beer. The other conversations around him were not revealing anything helpful, so he thought he'd finish his beer and leave Bat to it.

He stepped outside and saw the sheriff coming towards him.

"Adams," Sheriff Gaze said. "How's the investigation goin'?"

"I talked to the kids and the teachers," Clint said, "and Bat's running his own end of the investigation."

"How's he doin' that?"

"The best way he knows how," Clint assured the man.

Gaze nodded, and Clint hoped he wouldn't go inside the saloon and see Bat playing poker. He might misunderstand. As it turned out, he crossed the street and kept on walking.

***

An hour later Clint was sitting in The Sunflower Café when Bat Masterson came walking in. He spotted Clint and joined him at his table. The special, written on a chalkboard on the wall was beef stew, so they both ordered it.

"How was the game?" Clint asked.

"I made a few bucks," Bat said, "but came up with no information. How about you?"

"I talked with the teachers and the kids," Clint said. "It was a bust, except for this one boy, Roy."

"What about him?"

"He says he saw four riders, moving away from the train," Clint explained. "He couldn't describe them, didn't know how tall they were because they were on horseback."

"What about the horses?"

"Those he described," Clint said. "Two browns, a grey and a paint."

"A paint!" Bat said. "That's good. It's something we can look for. Good for Roy."

"Yeah," Clint said, "the teacher said he's got a vivid imagination, but I think this was on the level."

"Okay," Bat said, as the waiter set down their bowls, "after we eat, we can check out the livery stables. Do you know how many there are?"

"A few," Clint said. "We'll check them all."

Chapter Fifteen

After they finished eating, they walked the length of the town, intending to check every livery stable or barn, whether public or private.

They stopped in at every stall in the public liveries. They found plenty of browns, a few greys, but not one paint.

"Let's try these private barns," Bat said.

"They could have their horses in a barn outside of town," Clint suggested.

"We'll check them, too," Bat said. "It might take a lot of riding."

"We can split up."

"You think Willy, the conductor, can ride?"

"Not very well," Clint said, "but the sheriff would let us have his deputy."

"Good," Bat said, "the three of us can get it done much quicker."

"Let's finish with these private barns first"

***

They knocked on doors and asked to see the inside of several barns. They had to identify themselves to get the people to open the doors, but when they heard they were dealing with Clint Adams and Bat Masterson, they were glad to comply.

"Is this about the railroad wreck?" one man asked.

"Yes, it is," Bat said.

"I was one of the men who rode out there to help," the man said.

"I thought I recognized you," Clint said.

"That was a terrible thing to do, especially with children on board.

They looked around and didn't find a paint or a grey.

"What are you lookin' for?" the man asked.

They told him.

"I ain't seen a paint around here for a while," the man said. "But I seen a few greys."

"Yes, so have we," Clint said. "Thanks for your help."

"Sure thing," he said. "I hope you catch the bastards."

As they left the barn and the door closed behind them, Bat asked, "Do you think the bastards had time to ride back to town after the deed, and then volunteer to come out and help?"

"That would have taken some riding," Clint said. "But they might have been able to."

"Let's see if we can get that deputy from the sheriff for the morning," Bat said. "We can all ride out first thing. Finding that paint's going to be real helpful."

They stopped by the sheriff's office and told the man what they wanted.

"That's not a problem," Gaze said. "As a matter of fact, I have a couple of temporary deputies. I can give you them, also."

"That's great," Bat said. "With five of us, the work will go that much faster. We'll stop here early tomorrow and collect them."

"They'll be ready," he promised.

Clint and Bat left the office and stopped just outside.

"Want to get a beer?" Clint asked.

"Yes," Bat said, "but let's go somewhere other than The Oasis."

"Don't trust yourself to stay away from that poker game?" Clint asked.

"Not with Corbin there," Bat said. "He's pretty good."

"Did you know him before you came here?"

"No," Bat said, "just met him."

"There's a smaller saloon down the street," Clint said. "It's called Danny Dial's."

"Let's go," Bat said.

***

The went to Dial's for a beer each, standing at the bar with two other men. Several more were seated at tables. There were no poker games in progress.

"You two are strangers in town," the bartender said, setting their beers down. "You here because of that railroad thing?"

"That's right," Bat said. "You wouldn't know anything helpful, would you?"

"Hell, I wish I did," the bartender said. "There was kids on that train."

"You know anybody in town who rides a painted pony?" Clint asked.

"Naw, why?" the man asked. "Is that important?"

"Could be," Bat said.

"I'll keep an eye out for one," the man said. "Where can I find you?"

"The hotel down the street," Clint said, "or leave a message with the sheriff."

"Will do."

Bat took money from his pocket.

"Forget it," the bartender said. "It's on the house."

Chapter Sixteen

The gambler, Tom Corbin went to the bar for a beer, and stood next to a man named Jake Weller.

"You think it's smart to play poker with Bat Masterson?" Weller asked.

"Why not?" Corbin asked. "You know a better way to keep track of him?"

The men spoke without looking at or facing each other.

"Bad enough we got Masterson lookin' into this," Weller said, "but he's got Clint Adams helpin' him."

"Relax," Corbin said. "They don't know a thing."

"That's why they're askin' questions."

"They're not gonna find out anythin'," Corbin said. "Stop worryin'."

"We should be gettin' out of town," Weller said.

"I'm goin' back to my poker game," Corbin said. "Go to your room and stay there. You look nervous as hell."

Corbin left the bar and walked back to the poker table. Weller finished his beer and then walked nervously to the door and left the saloon.

***

When there was a knock on Clint's door, the last person he expected to see in the hall was Miss Rafferty.

"Miss Rafferty."

She stared at the gun in his hand.

"Do you always answer the door with a gun?"

"Yes," he said, "I'm afraid it's necessary."

"I see."

"But," he said, putting it behind his back, "obviously not now. What can I do for you, Miss Rafferty?"

"My name is Delores," she said, "and may I come in?"

He looked both ways in the hall.

"I'm not worried about my reputation if you're not worried about yours," she told him.

"All right," he said, backing away. "Come in."

She entered and he closed the door.

"Let me put this away," he said, indicating the weapon. He walked to the gunbelt hanging on the bedpost and holstered the gun, then turned to face her.

"I'm sorry," he said, "I don't have anything to offer you to drink."

"That's all right."

"Is this about the kids?" he asked.

"No, the kids are fine."

"Miss Long?"

She smiled and said, "She's fine, too."

"And are you okay?"

"I thought I was," she said.

"What happened?"

She shrugged.

"I met you."

"And that's a bad thing?"

"No," she said, "that's just it. Meeting you is a good thing."

"I'm glad to hear it."

They stood there staring at each other.

"Okay," he said, "What's so great about meeting me?"

She hesitated, then said, "I'm a teacher. I deal with children every day. The only adults are other teachers, and parents. And the only men are fathers."

"I'll bet the fathers like you," he said, "a pretty woman like you."

"Yes," she said, "some of them like me too much."

"So you have to fight them off?"

"Sometimes," she said, "but with you . . . I don't often meet a man I don't want to fight off."

"You know," he said, "I thought about inviting you to dinner."

"I don't think we have time for that," she said. "We might not be here very long, so I'm going to be bold. I hope that doesn't scare you off."

"No," he said, "I don't find bold women frightening, especially if they're pretty."

"So you think I'm pretty," she said. "That's the first step."

"And you don't want to fight me off," he said.

"Yes, please," she said. "I mean, no, I don't."

He crossed the room to her, bent and kissed her gently.

"Okay?" he asked.

"Very okay," she said.

This time when he kissed her, she put her arms around him, and the kiss went on for some time.

He drew back and stared at her.

"Can we get rid of these glasses?" he asked.

"I don't see why not," she said. He removed them and set them aside.

They kissed again and then she touched the buttons of his shirt and said, "And could we get rid of this?"

He smiled and said, "I don't see why not."

Chapter Seventeen

Delores Rafferty became less and less shy the more clothes that came off. She was slender and smooth, not exactly Clint's type, but she was sweet, nice, and smelled good. And she was eager.

When they both got naked and fell onto the bed together, she began to roam Clint's body with her hands, and mouth. He settled down onto his back to enjoy the attention and was surprised when the shy young teacher took his penis into her mouth. As she sucked him, he realized it wasn't the first time for her. So she had encountered men before who she didn't want to fight off. Possibly not for some time though.

She sucked him avidly and when he was almost ready to erupt, she backed off and kept him from finishing.

Clint flipped her over and began to explore her body in the same manner—hands, lips, tongue. Her breasts were small but firm, light colored nipples. Her skin was very smooth and fragrant, and when he settled his face between her legs, her nectar was sweet and slightly sticky. He lapped it up with great pleasure, and she writhed and moaned beneath his ministrations, her hands on his head to hold him in place, as if afraid he would stop too soon . . .

***

Lying side-by-side later, both of them tried to catch their breath.

"I knew I was right," she said.

"About what?"

"About us," she said, "that we should be together now, before it was too late."

"What about Miss Long?" he asked. "Should I bring her up here before you both leave—"

She slapped him on the arm and said, "No! She would be scandalized."

"Will you be here as long as the railroad's investigation takes?" he asked.

"I don't think so," she said. "I don't know why that would be necessary."

"It would probably be better for the children to go home," he said.

"This was just supposed to be a short field trip," she said. "They're going a bit stir crazy, being cooped up in that rooming house."

"Is Miss Peabody getting on their nerves?"

"No, she's wonderful with them," she said. "They love her."

"And her cookies, huh?"

"Oh yes . . ."

She rolled over against him.

"But I know something better than cookies," she said, running her hand down his body . . .

***

Delores hurried to get back to the rooming house before Miss Peabody locked her out.

Clint met Bat in the hotel lobby and they went directly to the sheriff's office. The lawman was there with three young men who wore deputy badges.

"This is Greg, that's Matt and you know my regular deputy, Ted Banner," Sheriff Gaze said, "Boys, this is Clint Adams, and that is Bat Masterson."

"It's a pleasure, Mr. Masterson," Banner said.

"You boys can use my office if you want, Gaze said. "I have early rounds."

"No," Bat said, "I think we'll take your deputies over to the Sunflower Café and buy them breakfast."

"Hey, that suits us," Matt said, and the other deputies nodded.

"Let's go then," Clint said. "We'll tell you what we expect of you as we eat."

"Thank you, Sheriff," Bat said.

The five men left the sheriff's office and walked to the café. The same waiter showed them to a table for five, near the back, and they all ordered.

While they ate, Clint and Bat told them what they were looking for.

"We're looking for a paint?" Matt asked.

"Or a paint and a grey," Bat said. "That would be even more of a giveaway. Maybe we can find two of them together."

"If any of you find that pony," Clint said, "ride right back to town and find one of us."

"Right," Banner said. "We got it, right boys?"

Matt and Greg nodded, and they finished breakfast. While they did, they split the county up so they wouldn't cover the same ground.

The deputies had walked their horses over from the sheriff's office. When they left the café, they mounted up and rode out. Clint and Bat walked to the livery stable to saddle their own horses.

They rode out of town together and when they got outside, separated to cover their own ground.

Chapter Eighteen

The area Clint took included five ranches and several homesteads. None of them were very large, but they all had barns, so he checked them all out. He was able to ride right up to some because no one was home. And because no one was home, the barns were empty.

Others he had to sneak up on, because the owners and a few hands were there. He wanted to get a look in the barns without anyone catching on. For the most part, that worked. And in each case, there was no grey and no paint.

He was in the last barn he would be checking that day. It was a small ranch which, from a distance, looked as if it was run by a husband-and-wife with no ranch hands. When he knew they were both in the house, he left his horse tied to a tree and made his way on foot to the barn. There was one horse, a dun, tied outside the front door. He waited a few moments to be sure no one came out of the house, then slipped into the barn, closing the door behind him. He had to be quick, because he didn't know if someone would be walking the horse in front of the house to the barn, or simply mount up and ride off somewhere.

The inside was dark, but he couldn't light a gas lamp that hung on a peg, so he waited for his eyes to acclimate. When they did, he saw several horses in stalls, one of which was lying on its side. He realized it was a mare in foal and was near her time. Someone in the house would be coming out soon to check on her.

He looked at the horses in the other stalls. There was a brown and a bay, but no paint. But there were a couple of other stalls that showed recent use. One could have been for the horse that was outside the house, but he would have liked to know who the other one was for.

The mare in foal made a loud sound, and Clint could see her belly was distended. He went to her and leaned over, laying his hand on her.

"Easy, girl," he said. "Someone will be in to help you."

His hand seemed to soothe her.

He heard a sound from outside and thought someone was bringing that horse to the barn. Instead, they mounted up and rode off. He figured maybe the husband was going for a vet.

He waited for the sound of the horse to fade, then went to the door to slip out. As he did, a woman's voice said, "Stop right there. I got a rifle pointed at you."

He froze.

"Go back inside," she said.

He did, and she followed.

"Light the lamp," she instructed.

He did.

"Turn around."

He did.

A tall, rangy woman in her forties, with a long angular face and stringy, graying hair was pointing a Winchester at him.

"Who are you?" she asked.

"My name's Clint Adams."

"Wait," she said, frowning, "I know that name. The Gunsmith, right?"

"That's right."

"What are you doing here?"

"I'm looking for some horses."

"Why?"

"Did you hear about the train crash nearby?"

"Yes, I did."

"I'm investigating it," he said. "We're looking for some horses that were ridden by the men who sabotaged the train."

"That crash was done on purpose?"

"Yes."

The mare whinnied then, a painful sound.

"Her time's near," he said.

She looked at the mare and said, “No, it’s here. My husband just went for the vet, but it’ll be a while before they get back.”

She lowered the rifle.

“Since you’re here, I’ll need your help,” she said.

“All right,” he said, “but first I need to ask you a question,”

“What?”

He pointed.

“Those two stalls, what horses were in there?”

“My husband’s dun,” she said.

“And the other?”

Another painful sound from the mare.

“I’ll tell you that,” she said, “but you have to help me with the mare first. She’s ready. I’m sure you’ve done this before.”

“A time or two.”

“Then let’s help her.”

He rolled up his sleeves and said, “Yes, let’s.”

“My name’s Claire,” she said. “I’ll go to the house and get some water. See if you can determine what position the foal is in.”

She set her rifle down and went out the door. Clint knelt by the mare.

Chapter Nineteen

The foal was turned the wrong way, but Clint and Claire managed to get it turned around, and they helped her deliver it. By the time her husband returned with the vet, the foal was on shaky legs, the mother cleaning it off.

"Who's this?" the husband asked.

"This is Clint Adams," Claire said. "He came by just as the mare was ready. He agreed to help me."

"I'll take a look at the mother and the foal," the vet said.

"Mr. Adams can come to the house to clean up," Claire said.

"I'll stay here with the foal," the husband said.

"Come with me, Mr. Adams," she said, picking up her rifle.

He followed the woman back to the house and she filled a basin with water for him to wash. Then she stood back and folded her arms.

"Your husband doesn't like that I'm here," he said.

"My husband doesn't like many people," she told him. "Don't worry about it."

He finished washing and turned to face her, drying his hands on a towel.

"I'll tell you about that other stall now," she said.

"You may not have to," he said.

"Why not?"

"The foal," he said. "It's a paint."

"Yes," she said, "we bred her to a paint."

"And it was in that stall?"

"For a while."

"Where is it now?"

"The owner took it back."

"When?"

"Long ago, after they mated."

"Is it near here?"

"The other side of the county," she said. "We let it be known we wanted to foal to a paint, and he came forward."

"What's his name?"

She looked out the window.

"My husband's comin'," she said. "He won't like me talkin' about this."

"Just tell me his name," Clint said.

"It's Boswell," she said, "Homer Boswell. He owns a big spread."

The door opened and her mouth clamped shut, and that was all he got. He didn't even learn her husband's name, or their last name.

***

As he rode away from the ranch, the husband and wife watched him. He knew the husband would have questions for Claire, such as why was Clint's horse so far from the house. She told him something, but nothing about the paint, so that Clint's questions wouldn't get back to Homer Boswell. But when Clint got to town, he would tell Bat about Boswell and they would check on his reputation.

There didn't have to be just one painted pony in the county, but this was a good start.

***

"That was Ed and Claire Holt," Sheriff Gaze told him. "He's a real hard case, doesn't like people."

"That's what she told me."

"They're good people, they just keep to themselves," the lawman said. "Now Boswell, that's a different story. Let me tell you . . ."

Chapter Twenty

Bat and the other deputies weren't back yet.

"One of the others probably checked the Boswell ranch," Gaze said. "It's a big spread. He's a respected rancher around here."

"Why would a man like that be involved in this?" Clint wondered.

Gaze shrugged.

"Maybe it's somebody who works for him."

"We'll find out if any of the others found a paint there," Clint said. "They should be back soon. I'm going to get a beer."

"I'll see you later," the sheriff said.

Clint left the man's office and went to The Oasis saloon. He saw Corbin in a poker game with some different players. He went to the bar and ordered a beer. Mug in hand, he turned and watched the poker game from a distance. It looked like Corbin was winning every two out of three hands.

At one point Corbin sat out and came to the bar, stood next to Clint.

"Your friends with Bat Masterson, right?" the gambler asked.

"That's right."

"Adams, right?"

"That's right."

"Lemme buy you another one."

"Sure."

Corbin waved to the bartender for two more.

"Have you seen Masterson lately?"

"Yes."

"I was hoping he was still in town," Corbin said. "I need some competition."

"I'm sure he'll be around."

"How about you?" Corbin asked. "I heard you're a pretty good poker player."

"I've had my moments."

"How about a few hands?"

"Not right now," Clint said. "But maybe later."

"Sure," Corbin said, "later."

He raised his mug to Clint, then walked back to the poker table.

The deputies began to arrive one at a time, first Banner, then Greg, and finally Matt. Clint bought them each a beer. None of them had visited the Boswell ranch.

The deputies had told Clint what they had found and left. Eventually, Bat appeared and joined Clint at the bar.

"They didn't find anything," Clint told Bat.

"It doesn't matter," Bat said. "I found a paint."

"At the Boswell ranch?"

Bat looked surprised.

"That's right. It's the only one I saw."

Clint told Bat about the foal at the Holt ranch.

"That doesn't have to be the only paint in the county," Bat said, "but we could go to the Boswell ranch and ask questions."

"Tomorrow?"

Bat nodded.

"I want to get this over with as soon as possible."

Clint glanced at the poker table and saw Corbin looking at them.

"Your poker buddy was looking for you," Clint said.

"He'll have to wait," Bat said. "I want to get this done."

"What about the teachers and the kids?" Clint asked. "Can we send them home?"

"I don't see why not," Bat said. "What about this foal?

"The Holts," Clint said. "The sheriff knows them. They stay to themselves. They let it be known they wanted to match their mare with a paint. Boswell responded and made his paint available."

"I might as well turn in, then," Clint said. "I'm pretty tuckered out from riding all day."

"How about a meal first?" Bat asked. "Over at that café?"

"Sounds good to me." Clint looked over and saw Corbin watching them. "You going to disappoint Corbin by walking out?"

"He'll wait," Bat said. "If he wants to play the best, he'll wait."

They finished their beer and walked out together.

***

Over a steak they discussed their next move, after the Boswell ranch.

"If the paint is there, it's no guarantee Boswell was involved," Clint said. "First we have to determine if it's the right horse, then whose horse it is."

"And finally," Bat said, "who rode the horse on that day."

"If it's a big ranch, it could have been anybody."

"We'll find out," Bat said.

"What about the train?" Clint asked. "Is the railroad going to clear that track?"

"Once I find out who was behind this, yes," Bat said. "But they'll leave it the way it is until I'm done."

“What about the train depot?” Clint asked. “Have you talked to the ticket clerk there? Or any of the other employees?”

“I’ll do that tomorrow, too,” Bat asked. “It shouldn’t take long. Just a few questions.”

“Want me to come along?”

“If you like.” Bat said. “Yeah, that’s a good idea. Then we can head to the Boswell ranch from there.”

“How do you intend to handle Boswell?” Clint asked.

Bat shrugged.

“We know there’s a paint on the grounds,” he said. “I’ll just ask him about it and see what he says.”

“You think you’ll be able to tell if he’s lying?” Clint asked.

“I can do it at a poker table,” Bat said. “I should be able to do it with him.”

“This’ll be interesting,” Clint said.

“You know,” Bat said, “one of your best friends is the best private detective in the country.”

“Talbot Roper.”

“Exactly,” Bat said. “So if you think of anything he might do, just let me know.”

“I will,” Clint said, “but up to now you seem to be doing all you can do.”

“I hope you’re right,” Bat said. “It’s been a long time since my railroad detective days.”

“You’ll make it work,” Clint assured him.

Chapter Twenty-One

In the morning Clint and Bat started with breakfast at the Sunflower Café. After that they walked to the railroad station to talk to the ticket clerk.

"I don't even know why I'm still here," the man said. "There's nothin' for me to do until the train runs again."

"You're here because you're still being paid," Bat said. "And that's the reason you're going to answer my questions."

"Of course," the clerk said. "I wanna help."

"What's your name?" Bat asked.

"Oswald," the middle-aged man said. "Folks call me Ozzie."

"Okay, Ozzie. Think back a few days, even a week before the train wreck. Was there anyone in here asking questions about the train, and its schedule."

"Well, lots of folk come in and ask about scheduling," Ozzie said. "That's part of my job, answerin' those questions. I didn't do nothin'—"

"Nobody's accusing you of anything, Ozzie," Bat said, cutting him off. "Just answer my questions."

"Yes, sir."

"Was anybody asking about this particular train?"

Ozzie frowned.

"I'm tryin' to remember," he said. "Nothin' specific comes to mind."

"Has anyone ever asked how far out of town the whistle can be heard?" Clint asked.

Bat looked pleased.

"Now that's a good question," he said. "I don't think the saboteurs would want the whistle to be heard." He looked at Ozzie. "What about it?"

"I do remember one man askin' me that," Ozzie said. "I really didn't know the answer though. I know I can hear the whistle as it approaches the station, but that's about it."

"Okay," Bat said. "Thanks."

They talked to some of the others who worked there. Most of them simply loaded and unloaded the cars, others did repairs on the station. No one was able to tell them anything helpful.

As they walked away from the station to the livery stable Clint said, "They could have sent somebody on horseback to find out where the whistle blew, and when, and then figure out if it could be heard from town."

"The whistle blows whenever the train crosses a road," Bat said. "It's supposed to warn wagons not to cross."

"The accident didn't happen at a crossing," Clint said.

"No, it was between crossings," Bat said. "All they had to do was time the train and listen for the whistles. Eventually, they'd decide which section of track to pry up. There are signals an engineer can blow to send for help. If they derail the train far enough from town, they couldn't get help. They were lucky you were riding by Clint. You probably saved a lot of lives."

"I just got them treated faster than they might've been," Clint said.

"And saved some lives," Bat repeated.

Clint shrugged.

"Maybe."

They reached the livery, saddled their horses and rode for the Boswell ranch.

***

The first time there Bat was able to get into the barn without being seen. This time, they rode right up to the house, where they were met by several men. The ranch and house were much larger than any of the others Clint had been to.

"Can we help ya?" one asked.

"We're here to see Mr. Boswell," Bat said.

"About what?"

"We just have some questions."

"Who are you?" a man asked.

"Who are *you*?" Bat replied.

"I'm Carl Maddox, the foreman."

"I'm Bat Masterson and this is Clint Adams."

"Masterson and the Gunsmith?" Maddox said. "What are you doin' here?"

"I'm an investigator for the railroad," Bat said.

"So this is about the train wreck?"

"Yes," Bat said.

"That's why you wanna see the boss?"

"Just to ask a few questions," Bat said.

"Wait here," Maddox said. "I'll go in and tell 'im."

"Thanks."

Maddox went into the house. The other hands who were with him walked away and scattered.

"Maddox is going to warn his boss," Clint said.

"Probably," Bat said, "but if Boswell's not involved, he's got nothing to worry about. This is just about a horse right now."

Clint nodded. The front door opened, and Maddox appeared. He waved for them to come in.

"He'll see you," he said. "Follow me."

They followed him inside, and he closed the door behind them.

Chapter Twenty-Two

"Mr. Masterson, Mr. Adams," a broad chested man with white hair greeted, "I'm Homer Boswell." He stood behind a desk and offered his hand. They both came forward and shook it.

"That's all, Carl," Boswell said to his foreman.

"Yes, sir." He left the room.

"Have a seat, please," Boswell said, sitting behind his desk.

Clint and Bat sat across from him.

"My foreman said this was about the train wreck?" Boswell asked.

"Kind of," Bat said. "Right now, it's more about a horse."

"A horse?" Boswell said. "I don't understand."

"We think one of the men who sabotaged the train tracks was riding a painted pony."

"What's that got to do with me?" Boswell asked.

"We heard a family named Holt wanted to breed their mare to a paint, and you had one."

"That's right, I do," Boswell said. "We let them breed, then took the horse back. It's nothing special, just one of our trail horses."

"We'd like to take a look at it, if we can," Bat said.

"I don't see why not," Boswell said, standing. "Come on, I'll walk you over to the barn."

They left the office together.

***

By the time they reached the barn Carl Maddox had joined them. He swung the doors open while they stood aside with Boswell.

"Go ahead in," Boswell said.

Maddox went in first. Bat entered, and Clint went in a couple of steps behind him, to watch his back, in case they were being ambushed. Boswell entered behind him.

The barn was very large, with many stalls. They found the paint in one toward the back.

"Here it is," Bat said.

He stepped into the stall while Clint remained outside, ready and aware. Bat inspected the animal's four hooves, touched it here and there and then backed out.

"It's a nice animal," he said. "Who owns it?"

"The ranch," Boswell said. "It doesn't belong to any one man."

"So anyone can ride it?" Clint asked.

"Yes," Boswell said. "My men own their own saddles, but not their own mounts."

"Is this horse in use a lot?" Bat asked.

"Pretty much," Boswell said, "right, Carl?"

"It's a popular mount with the men," Maddox said.

"Do you have any greys?" Bat asked.

"No," Maddox said. "Most of our mounts are brown or black."

Bat looked at Clint, waiting to see if he had any more questions. Clint shook his head.

"All right," Bat said. "Thanks, Mr. Boswell."

"Hey," Boswell said, "whatever I can do to help."

They all left the barn and walked to Bat and Clint's horses.

"If you have any more questions, come back and ask," Boswell said. "Anytime."

Bat nodded and said, "Thanks."

Clint and Bat rode away, with several ranch hands watching them go.

"Is this gonna be a problem?" Maddox asked Boswell.

"It shouldn't be," Boswell said. "But get the others together and let's talk about it."

"Yes, sir."

Boswell went back into the house.

***

When Clint and Bat had put some ground between themselves and the ranch, they reined in and looked behind.

"What'd you think?" Clint asked.

"If Boswell's lying, he's good at it," Bat said.

"And Maddox?"

"Oh, he's lying," Bat said. "Now I just have to figure out about what?"

"What about the horse?"

"It's got some distinctive marking on its right front hoof," Bat said. "I want to ride out to the wreckage and look around."

"That's good," Clint said. "If we can find that track then we'll know we've found the horse."

"Then all we have to do is find out who was riding it," Bat added.

Clint looked at the sky.

"We probably can't get to the wreckage before dark," he said.

"No," Bat said, "I was thinking of doing that some time tomorrow."

"That suits me," Clint said, and they rode back toward town.

Chapter Twenty-Three

When they got back to town, they took care of their horses and then had a simple meal in their hotel dining room. It wasn't as good as the café, but it did what it was supposed to do. They ate and talked.

"So you think we should concentrate on Maddox?" Clint asked.

"I do," Bat said, "whether we find that hoof print out there or not."

"Well," Clint said, "we can decide what to do after we ride out to the wreckage tomorrow."

Bat agreed. They finished eating and walked out to the lobby.

"It's a little early for me to turn in," Bat said. "I'm going to head over to The Oasis."

"Take a little of Corbin's money?" Clint asked.

"Maybe a lot of it, in a short time."

"Good luck."

"It's Corbin who's going to need the luck," Bat said.

"That's right," Clint said. "Look who I'm talking to."

"See you in the morning to go out to the wreckage," Bat said.

Bat went to The Oasis Saloon, and Clint went to his room.

***

Delores Rafferty and Miss Long had both left town with the children while Clint was out with Bat. There was no way for them to say goodbye or see each other again.

Clint had been turning in early to get up early and work with Bat. He decided to stay out of the saloons. He would drink too much, trying to listen to conversations around him, but they never revealed anything. Now he probably knew why. The saboteurs stayed out at the Boswell ranch, and out of the saloons.

For a moment he thought maybe he should go to the saloon and play poker with Bat, but then decided against it.

***

Corbin saw Bat come into the saloon and go to the bar. He ordered a beer and remained at the bar until he finished it. Then he walked to the poker table. Corbin knew Bat was going to play because he didn't have a drink in his hand. No matter what the stakes, Bat never drank while he played.

"Brought my money back to the table, huh?" Corbin asked.

"Just for a visit," Bat said. "To pick up a few friends."

The other players laughed, and one said, "It'll be nice to see the money go someplace else, for a change."

Corbin started to deal.

"How's your investigation into the wreck goin'?" he asked Bat.

"Slow," Bat said, and didn't elaborate.

During the course of the game Corbin kept bringing the wreck up, and Bat kept moving the subject away. Finally, Corbin stopped and just played poker, but it was too late. Bat had a feeling Corbin was in town for more than just poker.

***

In the morning, at breakfast, he told Clint what he suspected.

"If most of the men are out at the ranch, it makes sense to keep someone in town to keep an eye on things. That could be Corbin."

"If it is, he was sloppy," Bat said. "He was pushing too hard."

"Then maybe we should push back," Clint said. "Or else use him."

"To send phony information?" Bat asked. "That's not a bad idea."

They left the café to get their horses from the livery.

***

When they reached the wreckage site, they split up and began searching the ground for the hoof print left by the paint.

They rode back and forth along the wreckage, each time further and further away from the tracks. Finally, on a rise fifty yards from the scene, Bat saw some tracks, made by at least four horses. He dismounted to take a closer look, and then saw it, the hoof print they were looking for, in among the others. He drew his gun and fired one shot to get Clint's attention.

***

When Clint heard the shot, he knew Bat had found something. He stood in his stirrups and spotted Bat on a rise on the other side of the tracks.

As he rode toward it, he thought it looked like the spot where the child, Roy, said he saw the four riders.

Chapter Twenty-Four

When he reached Bat, he dismounted and joined him as the gambler pointed to the ground.

"That's it?" Clint asked.

"That's it," Bat said. "That cleft hoof. It's undeniable, that was the painted pony that was used by one of the men."

"So we're thinking that makes it undeniable that the riders—or, at least, that one—came from the Boswell ranch."

"And there's another thing that bothers me," Bat said.

"What's that?"

"The gambler, Corbin," Bat said. "He seemed to be very interested in my progress on this investigation last night, even moreso than poker. In fact, he lost quite a few hands because of his lack of attention."

"So why would he be interested, unless he was involved?"

"I should find out exactly when he got to town," Bat said.

"So we've got two directions to pursue," Clint said, "Boswell and Corbin."

"Let's get back to town," Bat said, grabbing his horse's reins, "and start pursuing."

***

When Carl Maddox brought Tom Corbin in to see Homer Boswell, the old man was not happy.

"What the hell are you doing here?" he demanded of the gambler.

"Don't worry," Corbin said, "nobody saw me comin' out of my house." He sat across from the man, who was seated behind his desk. "You gonna offer me a drink?"

"I want you to get to your business, and then get out of here," Boswell said. "The Gunsmith and Masterson have already been out here about that painted pony you insisted on riding."

"They can't prove anythin'," Corbin said. "Masterson played poker last night, and he had nothin'."

"How do you know?"

"I asked him."

Boswell's face grew red.

"Why the hell did you do that?" he demanded. "You probably gave away your involvement."

"Hey," Corbin said, "you're the one who wanted to get into the railroad business."

"My idea was a sound one," Boswell said. "You're making it harder by arousing Masterson's interest."

"He was too interested in poker," Corbin said. "Don't worry so much."

"Why shouldn't I worry?" Boswell yelled. "I'm the one with everything to gain and everything to lose. Where are the other men you used for this?"

"They're around," Corbin said. "It would be too suspicious for them to just disappear. Hell, two of them are your hands."

"And you should've checked with me before enlisting their involvement," Boswell said.

"Look," Corbin said, "the job got done, and I expect to get paid. So do my men."

"You'll get paid when this comes out the way I want it to."

"And when's that gonna be?"

"I'll let you know," Boswell said. "I just need you to stop taking chances like coming out here."

"Look," Corbin said, "I wanna move on—"

"Go ahead," Boswell said. "I'll know where you'll be and I'll send you your payment."

"That's not gonna work for me," the gambler said. "I'm not leaving town without my money."

"Then you'll have to be patient," Boswell said. "I need Bat Masterson to be gone."

"And what about Clint Adams?"

"Masterson's the one who works for the railroad."

"Well," the gambler said, "if you want him gone, that could be arranged."

Boswell hesitated for a moment, then took the time to light a cigar before asking, "Okay, what did you have in mind?"

"You should know," Corbin said, "this is gonna cost you extra."

***

Clint and Bat arrived back in town and took care of their horses.

As they left the livery Clint asked, "Do you want to bring the local law in on this?"

"I don't know," Bat said. "What do you think are the chances he's involved?"

"You're the one who claims he can read liars," Clint said, "but I don't think so. He seems straight to me."

"That was my first read," Bat said. "I guess we should keep him up to date on things."

"On facts or deductions?"

"We're not overloaded on facts," Bat said, "but I guess that would do."

In agreement then, they started for the sheriff's office.

Chapter Twenty-Five

Carl Maddox came in to see Homer Boswell after Corbin left.

"That man is going to be a problem," the rancher said.

"What do you want done about him?" Maddox asked.

"I haven't decided yet," Boswell said. "I still have a thing or two for him to do. But be ready, and I'll let you know."

"Yes, Sir."

The foreman left and Boswell relit his cigar. Masterson was his biggest problem, but it might just be remedied. He was going to have to wait and see.

***

Clint and Bat entered the sheriff's office, found him cleaning a rifle from his rack.

"Expecting trouble?" Clint asked.

"I like to be ready," Gaze said. "One never knows."

"That's true," Bat said.

"I'll bet you two aren't here with good news," he said, putting the rifle back in the rack.

"That depends on what you consider good news," Bat said.

Gaze leaned back in his chair.

"Let me have it," he said.

Clint let Bat tell Gaze about their visit to Boswell's ranch, and their ride out to the wreckage.

"So you found one of the horses," the lawman said.

"But not who was riding it," Clint added.

"Somebody from Boswell's ranch," Gaze said, "but not him."

"Why not?" Clint asked.

"He's a rancher," Gaze said. "Why would he have anythin' to do with this?"

"Bat doesn't think he's involved either," Clint said, "but he's already said his ranch owns the horse."

"It could have been any of his hands," Gaze said.

"I suppose so," Clint said.

"Okay, what if he is involved?" Bat asked. "What's his next move going to be?"

"Maybe get rid of that horse," Clint said.

"So what's the plan?" Gaze asked.

"Well, one of us should watch Corbin," Bat said. "I guess that would be me, at the poker table."

"Then I'll watch Boswell and the ranch," Clint said, "see if they move that horse."

"What about my deputies?" Gaze asked. "Need them to watch anyone?"

"Banner can help me watch the ranch," Clint said. He looked at Bat. "I don't think we need the other two."

"No, I agree."

"All right, then," Gaze said. "Banner's yours. I'll have him here in an hour. Let me know if you need anything else."

"We will," Clint promised.

Bat and Clint left the office.

"I'll pick up Banner later and get him placed," Clint said.

"I'll sit in tonight at the Oasis, see what Corbin has to say."

"You won't ask him anything, right?"

"Obviously," Bat said, "and depending on how much he asks me, it might mean he spoke to the others after we talked last night."

"Bat," Clint said, "they may come after you."

"Or you," Bat said.

"You're the one who works for the railroad," Clint said. "They'll come for you first."

"And if they get me?"

Clint patted Bat on the back and said, "Then I'll get them."

"I'd rather have this end some other way."

"So would I."

"I'll pick Banner up in an hour and see you later."

"At The Oasis," Bat said, "but don't come near the poker table. Stay at the bar."

"Right."

Bat headed for The Oasis, while Clint walked to Danny Dial's Saloon.

***

Bat was almost to The Oasis door when the first shot came. He was moving when the second one came, and then rolled away just ahead of the third and fourth. There was obviously more than one shooter.

When Bat hit the ground he drew his gun, took cover behind a horse trough, and tried to locate the shooters.

***

Clint heard the first shot, whirled and started running toward it. As shots followed, he hoped he would get there in time to help Bat out of a jam.

Chapter Twenty-Six

Clint ran for The Oasis because that was where Bat was headed. People were running in the street to get away from the flying lead.

Clint spotted a shooter right away. He fired before the man even knew he was there. The bullet took the man in the throat, killing him immediately.

He located Bat, who had taken cover behind a trough. From what Clint could see there were two more shooters across the street. Bat saw him and, knowing he had back-up, stood up.

The shooters saw Clint, then saw Bat stand up and, knowing they were outgunned, panicked. One began firing, but the other turned to run. Clint shot the one pulling the trigger, and Bat got the other as he was fleeing.

They came together over the first man Clint had shot.

"They rushed it," Bat said. "I'm lucky they didn't know what they were doing."

They split up and checked all three bodies as the sheriff came running up.

"What the hell happened?"

“They tried for Bat sooner than we thought,” Clint said. “We had just split up.”

“He’s lucky you’re a fast runner.”

“And a good shot,” Clint said.

“Do you know these fellas?” Bat asked Gaze.

The lawman took the time to turn them all over, then stood up straight.

“Well, I think this confirms it for you.”

“What do you mean?” Bat asked.

Gaze pointed.

“That one’s name is Harrigan,” Gaze said. “He’s a Boswell hand. Or, at least, he was at one time.”

“Not anymore?” Clint asked.

“I can’t be sure, but like I said, he was. I don’t know the other two.”

“So there’s a connection,” Bat said, “or there was. It’s not quite confirmed.”

“I can go to Boswell and ask him about Harrigan, see if he still worked there,” Gaze said. “See how he reacts to this.”

“That’s a good idea,” Bat said.

Gaze looked at the people lining the streets.

“I’ll get some of these good citizens to get their bodies off the street.”

“What’ll your approach to Boswell be?” Bat asked.

"I'll ask him if he wants to cover Harrigan's funeral expenses," Gaze said.

"That sounds good."

"Did he have any family you know of?" Clint asked.

"From what I knew of him, no," Gaze said. "He was single."

Gaze walked away to get some men to move the bodies. Clint saw some faces looking over the batwing doors.

"Is Corbin at the door watching?" he asked.

"No."

"Either he's not interested," Clint said, "or he knew what was happening."

"Then he won't be happy when I walk into The Oasis," Bat said.

"You still going to play poker with him?"

Bat grinned.

"More than ever."

"I'll pick up Banner and get him placed at the ranch," Clint said. "This mess might force someone to make a move."

"Let's hope it does," Bat said. "This shows a little desperation on somebody's part."

"Let's hope for a big mistake," Clint said.

Bat started to walk away, but Clint put his hand on his arm.

"You sure you don't want me to come in with you?"

"I'll be fine," Bat said. "You just watch yourself."

"I will," Clint said.

***

When Clint got to the sheriff's office, the lawman wasn't back yet, but Deputy Banner was there.

"What was all that about?" the young man asked.

"Somebody tried to bushwhack Bat."

"Did you bail him out?"

"We took care of things," Clint said. "Bat's fine."

"Glad to hear it," Banner said. "So what do we do?"

"Let's get your horse," Clint said. "We're going to ride out to the Boswell ranch, and I'll fill you in on the way."

"Good," Banner said, "I wanna be involved. Those bastards hurt a lot of kids."

"Yes, they did," Clint said.

***

By the time they came within sight of the ranch, Clint had filled Banner in on everything he knew.

"It's going to be dark soon," Clint said. "Stay aware, because they might move the horse then."

"Do I follow?"

"Yes," Clint said, "we'll want to know where that horse is. Just make sure you're careful, and no one sees you."

"They won't."

"And if you find out anything, let us know as soon as you can."

"Right."

"And don't get any closer," Clint said, "no matter what."

"Gotcha."

With Banner in place, Clint headed back to town.

Chapter Twenty-Seven

When Clint got back to town it was full dark. He left his horse at the livery and went directly to The Oasis. When he entered, he looked over at the poker table, saw Corbin and Bat sitting across from each other. He walked directly to the bar and ordered a beer.

Beer in hand, he kept his eyes on the poker table, using the mirror behind the bar. From the looks of things at the moment, the only talking that was being done was to call their plays. It didn't look like there was any real conversation going on.

As it got later, players left the game one-by-one, until there was only Bat and Corbin left. Clint was wondering how long they would stay at it, but soon, after that thought, they gave it up. Clint waited to see if they would exchange any words before leaving, but Corbin pocketed his money and walked out. Once he was gone, Bat joined Clint at the bar.

"Win?" Clint asked.

"Of course," Bat said, waving at the bartender for a beer. "What do you think?"

"Any other conversation?"

"In the beginning I think Corbin was surprised to see me walk in," Bat said. "He started asking questions, but I gave him one-word answers. Eventually, he stopped. I think the others at the table felt the tension between us, because they stayed quiet, except for the game."

"Well, if they felt it and they're not involved, then he obviously feels it."

"I'm sure he does."

"And you're sure the other players at the table aren't plants?"

"No, they're mostly storekeepers and businessmen from town."

"Well, if the tension's that obvious, maybe it's time to confront Corbin."

"What about the deputy?"

"He's in place," Clint said. "If he finds out anything, he'll let us know."

"And are we sure he's not a plant?" Bat asked.

"No, he's not," Clint said. "He's young and he wants to help. And the sheriff trusts him."

"And you trust the sheriff."

"Right."

"Well, let's see if the kid finds out anything before we confront Corbin."

"Then we're done for the night," Clint said.

"Soon as I finish this beer, I'm turning in," Bat said.

"I'll wait for you," Clint said. "We'll walk back to the hotel together."

"Fine," Bat said. "We'll put each other to bed."

***

It was dark when Deputy Banner saw somebody walk the painted pony out of the barn. He couldn't tell who it was from that distance, but he was sure he could follow them without being seen. He mounted up and waited.

The paint wasn't saddled. The hand brought another saddle horse out, mounted it, grabbed the lead of the pony and rode off.

Banner waited to see what direction the rider and horse went, and then followed. Moving slowly, and leading the pony, the men would be moving slow and would be easy to trail, even in the dark.

***

The ranch hand led Banner to a box canyon they were apparently using for some horses. Maybe the animals had been used by the riders who sabotaged the train. He couldn't say for sure because he never saw them, but he had been told about the painted pony, and there it was.

The box canyon was about ten miles out of town, in the opposite direction of the wreckage. They would have had to ride ten miles from the train to bring the horses here. Maybe they had fresh mounts waiting.

Banner dismounted and moved closer to the canyon on foot after securing his horse. He just wanted a closer look.

He got to the mouth of the canyon, and heard the sound of horses, but didn't hear anyone talking. He assumed the rider was there alone, leaving the pony among a few others.

He kept moving and eventually saw some light ahead. It seemed like lit torches. He was going to keep moving toward them when he heard something behind him.

"Just stand still," a voice said.

Banner froze.

"Take your gun out and drop it on the ground."

Banner slid the gun from his holster.

"Don't think about it."

But he did think about it, and it caused him to hesitate.

"Shit," the man behind him said, and pulled the trigger.

The bullet punched Banner square in the back and dropped him.

"What the hell?" the other hand yelled as he came running, carrying a torch.

"You were followed," the shooter said. "I came up behind him and he went for his gun. His horse is down the trail."

"Who is he?"

"I don't know," the shooter said. "Let's have a look."

They both leaned down to turn him over, and when they did, the light from the torch reflected off his deputy's badge.

"Oh, shit," they both said.

Chapter Twenty-Eight

When Bat entered his room, Clint walked down the hall to his. Because of what had happened to Bat, he opened his door real quietly and slipped in. The oil lamp on the bedside table was burning, and Delores Rafferty looked at him from the bed and smiled. She was naked beneath the sheet.

"What the hell are you doing here?" he asked.

"That's not a very nice greeting," she said, "I thought I'd surprise you."

"Well, you did," Clint said, lifting his gun. "You almost got shot."

"I—I'm sorry," Miss Rafferty said. "I was hoping you'd be glad to see me." She pulled the bedsheet up to her shoulders and looked embarrassed.

"Oh, hey, look," he said, holstering his gun and sitting next to her on the bed. "I am glad to see you. I was just surprised. I thought you took the kids home—to wherever that is."

"Miss Long agreed to take them home," she said. "I wanted to spend more time with you."

"I appreciate that."

He leaned over and kissed her, then stood, removed his gunbelt and hung it on the bedpost.

"Well then," she said, reaching for him, "let's make the most of the time we have."

"Agreed," he said, unbuttoning his shirt . . .

***

Clint made sure there was a chair jammed beneath the doorknob before getting into bed with Miss Rafferty. Once between the sheets, and wrapped in her arms and legs, he forgot about everything else for a short time.

Since he hadn't expected to ever see her again, he decided to take full advantage of their time together. He enjoyed her lovely body as much as he could without causing her to scream out loud, and by the time he was finished she was panting as if she had run a mile.

"My God," she gasped, "that was certainly worth coming back for."

"How far did you get?" Clint asked.

"I went with Miss Long and the kids in a couple of rented buckboards, until the next town with a train station. Then I decided to turn around and come back."

"And where are they going?" Clint asked. "Where's home?"

“Amarillo,” she said. “Not far, at all. I’ll be able to get back in a couple of days.”

“Can Miss Long handle all the kids while you’re gone?”

“The kids are on vacation, really,” she said. “That’s why I was able to get away. But I’ll get back by the time classes start again.”

“When will that be?”

“A couple of days,” she said. “Is that all right?”

“Sure,” he said, “but I don’t know how much time I can spend with you. I’m trying to help Bat with this investigation.”

“I understand,” she said. “I’ll take whatever time you can give me.”

She snuggled in close to him, and they went to sleep.

***

The two men dragged Deputy Banner’s body into the canyon and took the time to bury him. Then they went out to get his horse.

“Where is it?” Ron Kitterick asked.

“It was right here,” George Tice said.

“Goddamned,” Kitterick said. “You shouldn’t’ve shot ’im.”

“It’s a little late for that now,” Tice said. “Let’s mount up and see if we can find it. If we don’t, we’re gonna have to tell the boss.”

***

They spent two hours looking for Banner's horse, then had no choice but to head back to the Boswell ranch. They put their horses in the barn.

When they walked up to the house Kitterick asked, "Should we tell Mr. Boswell?"

"You wanna tell 'im?" Tice asked.

"Hell, no!"

"Then we better tell Maddox and let him tell Boswell," Tice said.

"There's gonna be trouble when that deputies horse gets back to town without him."

"Maybe they'll think he got thrown," Tice said. "This might even work for us."

"How do you figure that?"

"They might send out a search party for him," Tice said, "which means they'll stop workin' on the train wreck."

Kitterick thought that over and said, "What if we don't tell anybody about the deputy? I mean, they ain't gonna find 'im. And we'll be in less trouble."

Tice looked at Kitterick and said, "I'm in favor of that."

"Okay, then," Kitterick said, "let's get some sleep and see what happens in the mornin'."

Chapter Twenty-Nine

Clint woke in the morning with Miss Rafferty lying with her bare back to him. He wished he had time for her that morning, but he had to meet Bat downstairs. He got dressed and left without waking her.

"Did you get any sleep?" Bat asked. "You look terrible."

"I slept," Clint said. "Why don't we just have a quick breakfast here?"

"Why not?"

They were in the middle of breakfast in the hotel's half dining room when Sheriff Gaze came rushing up to their table.

"What is it?" Clint asked. "What's wrong?"

"Banner's horse came back during the night without him," Gaze said.

"He might have been thrown during the night," Bat suggested.

"Or they spotted him. They could've taken him or killed him."

Bat and Clint stood.

"We'll help you look for him," Bat said.

"We'll have to start at the ranch."

The three of them rushed out of the hotel to the livery stable to saddle their horses. As they walked the horses out and prepared to mount, Clint stopped them.

"What?" Bat asked.

"I've got an idea," Clint said. "I know the tracks are days old, but we found that painted pony's hoof print. We should have followed it. We can do it now. It might lead us someplace they're using as a hideout. Maybe they've got Banner there."

"Okay, you do that," Gaze said. "I'll get my other two men and we'll look for Banner."

"Or we could drag Corbin from his hotel room and make him talk," Bat said.

"Beat it out of 'im?" Gaze asked.

"Why not?" Bat asked.

"We've got five men," Gaze said. "Clint can track the prints, you can push Corbin and I'll go out and look for Banner. What do we do with the fourth and fifth man?"

"You take them," Bat said. "You'll cover more ground that way."

"You guys are okay alone?" Gaze asked.

"Don't worry about us," Bat said. "We're used to working alone."

"Then let's get goin'," Gaze said.

They all mounted up and rode in separate directions.

***

Bat rode directly to the hotel Tom Corbin was staying in. He dismounted, rushed into the lobby to the front desk. The clerk looked startled.

"What room is Tom Corbin in?"

"He's in one-oh-five," the young man said, "but he doesn't like to be woke up. He plays poker til late."

"Don't worry about it," Bat told him.

He ran up the stairs to room one-oh-five and kicked in the door. Corbin was in the act of getting dressed. He whirled, saw Bat and dove across the bed for his gun. Bat wanted him alive and hesitated, but as Corbin's hand closed around the butt of his pistol, Bat had no choice but to draw and fire.

***

Gaze found his two part time deputies, Greg and Matt, and told them to get their horses.

"What's goin' on, Sheriff?" Matt asked.

"Ted's in trouble," the lawman said. "We've got to find him."

"What kind of trouble?" Greg asked.

"Just get your horses and I'll tell you on the way."

***

Clint rode the Tobiano hard out to the site of the wreck. He found the painted pony's cleft hoofprint again, got off his horse and walked a few yards. The print was in among three more, but it stood out. He mounted up again and started to track it.

He lost the prints several times on hard scrabble ground but picked it up again as he kept riding. Once he thought he had lost it for good, and wished he was a better tracker. The young deputy's life could be in danger.

He hoped Bat and Gaze were having better luck.

***

Bat dragged the bleeding gambler through the lobby to the front door and out. Once there, he dragged him to the doctor's office.

When he got to the door, he banged on it with one hand while holding Corbin up with the other. The bullet had taken him in the shoulder, and it needed tending.

When the doctor opened the door Bat said, "You've got to keep this man alive!"

Chapter Thirty

Sheriff Gaze and his two deputies got to the Boswell ranch and viewed from afar.

"What was he doin' out here alone?" Greg asked.

"He was supposed to be watchin', and that's all," Gaze said.

"Hey, you know Ted," Matt said. "He's a hard head."

"Well," Gaze said, "it may have cost him this time."

"So whatta we do?" Greg asked. "Go down and talk to them."

"They'll just lie," Gaze said. "And Boswell's an important man around here."

"So where's that leave us?" Greg asked.

"We keep lookin' for him," Gaze said. "Let's see if we can pick up some tracks."

"You know what Ted's horse's tracks look like, Sheriff?" Matt asked.

"No, but Adams and Masterson told me about a horse with a cleft hoof," Sheriff Gaze said. "We're gonna look for that and track it."

"Where do we start?" Greg asked.

Gaze scowled and said, "Good question."

***

Clint found the print again and continued to follow it. At one point the four prints split up. As the cleft print veered west, Clint decided it was going to the Boswell ranch. But they already knew that the painted pony was there. What they wanted to know was where it was now.

Another track headed north, while two maintained their path to the east. If Clint had more riders they could split up and follow all three, but he was going to have to choose one.

He decided against following the cleft hoof back to the ranch. That meant he had to go north or east. He decided to follow the trail of the two riders and headed east. He crossed no other tracks along the way, so was never in danger of losing the trail. He was able to follow the tracks right to the mouth of a box canyon.

He decided against riding right straight in and decided to go in on foot. He looked for a likely place to tie off his horse, and when he found it, noticed tracks of a horse that had been tied there recently.

Maybe even last night.

***

"How is he?" Bat asked the doc when he came out of his exam room.

"He'll live, but he ain't talkin' for a while," the doctor said. "Right now, he's unconscious."

"He's got to talk," Bat said. "The deputy's life might depend on it. You've got to do something to wake him up."

"I can try," the doc said, with a sigh, "but I don't know how long he'll stay awake, or if he'll make any sense."

"We've got to try it," Bat said.

The doc shrugged again and said, "Have it your way."

***

Clint walked into the box canyon, found a makeshift corral with several horses in it, including the paint. There were no men there, so he was able to walk around. Eventually, he found a fresh grave. He felt fairly certain he had found Deputy Ted Banner.

The questions were: who put these horses here, and how long would he have to wait for someone to show up so he could find out?

That was when he heard some horses approaching, and took cover, hoping they wouldn't spot his Tobiano outside the canyon.

***

The sheriff and his deputies split up, then came together again.

"What's that?" Greg asked, pointing.

"Looks like tracks," Gaze said. "Several different horses."

"Goin' where?" Matt asked.

"That's what we're gonna find out," Gaze said.

They followed the trail and eventually came to what looked like the entrance to a box canyon.

"Whataya think, Sheriff?" Greg asked.

"A likely place for a hideout," Gaze said, "or a place to keep some horses. Let's take a look. Greg, keep watch out here."

"Yes, sir."

"Stay alert, Greg."

They directed their horses into the canyon.

***

Clint saw two men ride in slowly. When he recognized them, he stepped forward with his hands out, showing that they were empty.

"Fancy meeting you boys here," he said.

Chapter Thirty-One

"What the hell—" Sheriff Gaze said, as he and Matt dismounted. "I didn't think we'd end up in the same place."

"Where's your other deputy?" Clint asked.

"Outside, keepin' watch."

"Good." Clint pointed. "There's a paint in that corral."

"The one we're lookin' for?" Gaze asked.

"Let's take a look," Clint suggested.

The three men walked to the corral. Clint went in among the four horses and took a look at the pony's hoof.

"This is him," he said.

"Any sign of Banner?" Gaze asked.

"I think so," Clint said. "There's a fresh grave over there."

"Goddamnit!"

"You wanna dig 'im up to make sure, Sheriff?" Greg asked.

"No," Gaze said, "but we may have to."

"I was just thinking it could be quite a while before somebody came by here again."

"We can't wait that long," Gaze complained.

"Well," Clint said, "we know where the horses are, and nobody knows we do."

"And we found Banner, goddamnit," Gaze said.

"We might as well go back to town and see what Bat's found out from Corbin."

The sheriff and deputy walked their horses out with Clint, joined Greg, and then walked to Clint's horse and watched him mount up.

"I'm sorry about the deputy," Clint said, "but I think we're getting closer to finding out who's behind this whole thing."

"When we do," Gaze said, "I'm gonna toss their ass in jail so fast it'll make their head spin!"

"Even if it's Mr. Boswell?" Greg asked.

"Especially if it's Homer Boswell!" Gaze said, viciously.

***

So far, all Bat had got from Corbin was some feverish babbling.

"This shoulder wound doesn't look that bad," Bat complained to the doctor. "What's wrong?"

"He's lost a lot of blood, and he's feverish," the doctor said. "You might have to wait for the fever to break before he makes any sense."

"Damn it!" Bat snapped. "I'll be at The Oasis. Let me know as soon as he can talk."

"I might have other patients—"

"Doc, this man might be responsible for the death of Deputy Banner," Bat said. "The sheriff is going to want to know as soon as he can talk."

"All right," the doctor said, "but if I get an emergency—"

"Yes, yes," Bat said, and left the office.

As he walked to the saloon it was dusk. He felt he had wasted his whole day and hoped that Clint and the sheriff had better luck. He felt like a fool for shooting the gambler, but the man had given him no choice.

That didn't make him feel any better.

***

As Clint and the lawmen rode back into town, it felt too quiet for any kind of violence to have erupted in the street while they were gone.

"Let's find Bat," Clint said, dismounting.

"Greg," the sheriff said, "take the horses to the livery, then you and Matt can go have some dinner."

“Thanks, Sheriff,” Greg said, and both deputies rode to the livery.

“Where would Bat be?” Gaze asked.

“Where else?” Clint asked. “The Oasis.”

***

Bat saw Clint and Gaze as soon as they entered. He was sitting alone at a table with a beer, dealing out solitaire.

“You don’t look happy,” Clint said.

Bat scowled.

“Corbin went for his gun as soon as he saw me,” Bat said. “He left me no choice.”

“Is he dead?” Clint asked.

“He’s at the doc’s,” Bat said. “We’re waiting for his fever from a shoulder wound to break.”

“Have a seat and fill ’im in,” the sheriff said. “I’ll get some fresh beers.”

By the time the sheriff returned with three frosty mugs, Bat knew the whole story.

“Well,” the gambler said, “at least we know where the horse is. And those other horses must’ve been ridden by the other men.”

"Four men were seen riding away from the wreck," Clint said. "But there's got to be more involved. Three already tried to kill you."

"And Boswell," the sheriff said. "So that's at least seven."

"And Corbin makes eight," Clint said.

"Let's go with our original plan, go out and see what Boswell has to say about one of his men trying to kill me, with two others."

"It's already dark," Gaze said. "Let's do that tomorrow. I also want to get some boys to go out in a buckboard and bring Banner's body back."

"Sheriff," Bat said, "I think that should wait until we clear this all up."

"Sure," Gaze said, sourly, "it ain't like he's goin' anywhere."

Chapter Thirty-Two

Clint, Bat and Gaze had a meal at the café. Bat was upset he had shot Corbin, Gaze was depressed by the apparent death of his deputy. Clint was just upset by the whole situation.

Abruptly, Bat dropped his utensil noisily onto his plate.

"I'm going to check on Corbin at the doc's," he said. "After that I'll be in The Oasis."

He got up and left.

"I'm surprised by one thing," Clint said to Gaze.

"What's that?"

"That nobody seems to be trying to solve the death of Ted Banner."

"There's always a chance that when we dig up that grave tomorrow, it won't be him."

"What are the chances of that?"

Gaze scowled and said, "I know."

"I can't believe killing a lawman was planned," Clint said. "Banner probably walked in on something and got himself killed. If it wasn't planned, the men who did it might be trying to hide it."

"And the horse got away and ran back to town. So maybe Boswell doesn't know about it."

"We're going to find out tomorrow if he knows about the attempt on Bat," Clint said. "Let's see if he knows about Banner's death."

"Tell me why a man like Boswell would be involved in this train wreck?"

"He's a businessman," Clint said. "If he's looking to get into the railroad business, he might be trying to take over an existing business."

"By sabotagin' their track?"

"That could be the start of a campaign that's meant to drive them out of business," Clint said. "Or, at least, into a situation where they have to sell."

"What have the conductor and fireman been doin' in town?" the lawman asked.

"I haven't spoken to either one since Bat arrived," Clint said.

"Do we even know if they're still in Dexter?" Gaze asked.

"That might be something else we need to find out tomorrow," Clint said. "I never thought one of them was involved."

"If one was, it'd be the fireman, right?" Gaze said. "The conductor would have no effect on the engine."

"That's true," Clint said. "The fireman, Lester, was injured, but he could have done that himself."

"If Boswell's lookin' to take over the business, he'd probably need some inside help."

"That's true."

Clint frowned. Just when it seemed things might be becoming clearer, they were getting muddied again. Clint needed to talk to Bat about his friend, who owned the railroad.

He pushed his plate away.

"I'm going to check in with Bat at The Oasis," he said.

"I'll be in my office," Gaze said, and the two men stood up and left.

***

Bat stopped at the doctor's office and found no change in Corbin's condition. He went from there to The Oasis. He was sitting at a table dealing solitaire when Clint walked in.

Clint got a beer from the bar and joined Bat. He told his friend about his conversation with the sheriff.

"If there's an inside man at the railroad," Bat said, "it's not William Reynolds. He's not about to sabotage his own company."

"He's your friend," Clint said. "You ought to know."

"However," Bat said, "he does have board members."

"One of them could be in league with Homer Boswell."

"Maybe you better send your friend a telegram tomorrow."

"Yes," Bat said, "I'll ask him to have another investigator look into his board."

"Good idea."

"I'll get on that tomorrow."

"We've got a busy day tomorrow," Clint said.

"You're right," Bat said. "There's no point in sitting around here all night. We might as well turn in and get an early start tomorrow. We can help the sheriff recover his deputy's body before we visit Boswell." They both stood up. "And I can send that telegram to William in Amarillo."

"The railroad office is in Amarillo?"

"Yes," Bat said, "I didn't mention that before?"

"No, you didn't."

"Does that mean anything to you?"

"I don't know," Clint said, "but I'm going to find out."

***

Clint's intention was to go to his room and talk to Delores Rafferty about Amarillo, but the woman wasn't there.

He wondered just how much of this plot was hatched in Amarillo?

Chapter Thirty-Three

When he woke the next morning, Clint was surprised that Miss Rafferty hadn't returned to his room. After all, she had talked about wanting to spend a lot of time with him. He was suddenly suspicious about both her and Lester, the fireman. But then, he was kind of suspicious about everyone, except for Bat and the sheriff. He was not even as sure about Bat's friend as the gambler was.

He met Bat in the lobby and, once again, they had a quick bite in the dining room. At that point, meals were just a formality.

"I'll check on Corbin at the doctor's office and meet you at the sheriff's," Bat said.

"Fine."

They split up outside the hotel.

***

Clint walked into the sheriff's office, found him there with his deputies.

"We ready to go?" Gaze asked.

"Bat's checking on Corbin, then he'll meet us here and we can get our horses."

"Good," Gaze said. He looked at his deputies. "You boys go and get a buckboard."

"Yes, sir." The two young men left the office. "What's on your mind?" he asked Clint.

"Does it show?" Clint told the lawman about the conversation he had with Bat the night before.

"So he'll send that telegram before we leave today?" he asked.

"Probably doing that now."

"What else?"

So he told Gaze the rest, about the railroad office being in Amarillo and the teacher being from Amarillo.

"What would a young schoolteacher have to do with all this?"

"I have no idea," Clint said.

"Maybe you're just gettin' suspicious of everybody," Gaze suggested.

"Except for you and Bat."

"I appreciate that."

Bat entered the office at that point.

"Send your telegram?" Clint asked.

"I did."

"And how's Corbin?" Gaze asked.

"Still unconscious."

"All right, then," Gaze said, rising. "We might as well get horses and start movin'."

The three men left the office together.

***

Carl Maddox walked into his boss' office.

"Is that horse gone?" he asked the foreman.

"Yes, sir," Maddox said. "It's in the box canyon with the others."

"That idiot gambler," Boswell said. "First that stupid pony, and now he gets three men killed trying to bushwhack Masterson. I expect the sheriff to show up here today with Masterson, and maybe Adams."

Maddox frowned.

"You're not expectin' us to take care of them, are you?"

"Hell, no," Boswell said. "I'm not sending a bunch of cowhands after the Gunsmith and Bat Masterson. I'll take care of them myself."

"How will you do that?"

"They're an idiot lawman and two gunfighters," Boswell said. "I don't think I'll have trouble talking circles around them. Just bring them in when they get here."

"Yes, sir."

"You can go now."

Maddox left the office and the house.

***

When Clint, Bat, the sheriff and his two deputies reached the box canyon, they left Matt outside on watch. The rest went in to retrieve the body of Ted Banner.

They had only brought two shovels with them, so they took turns digging up the grave. When they had uncovered the body, there was no doubt it was the deputy.

"He was shot in the back," Gaze grumbled.

They wrapped the body in a blanket and set it on the bed of the buckboard.

"Matt," Gaze said, "you take him to the undertaker. The rest of us are goin' to the Boswell ranch."

"Yes, sir."

"If we don't come back," Gaze said, "it'll be up to you to find out why."

Matt swallowed and said, "Yes, sir." Then he drove the buckboard out of the canyon and headed for town.

"Okay," the sheriff said, "the Boswell ranch."

"Wait," Clint said, "I have an idea."

He rode back into the canyon as the others waited, then came out leading the paint.

"Good idea," Bat said.

"Okay," Clint said, "let's go."

Chapter Thirty-Four

When they reached the Boswell ranch, they were watched by some of the hands as they approached and met by the foreman, Maddox.

"What can I do for you boys?" the foreman asked.

"We wanna see Mr. Boswell," the sheriff said.

"What's it about?" Maddox asked.

"How about a wrecked railroad and a dead deputy?" Bat asked.

"Not to mention a dead hand of yours who tried to kill Bat," Clint said.

The door to the house opened, and Homer Boswell stepped out.

"What is this nonsense?" he demanded.

"Maybe you wanna go and talk about this in your office, Boswell?" the sheriff asked.

"No," Boswell said in a rough tone, "I don't want any of you in my house. Say what you have to say right where you are."

"One of your men, named Harrigan, tried to kill Bat Masterson with two other men. What have you got to say to that?" the sheriff asked.

"I'm sure it's not the first time Mr. Masterson's been shot at," Boswell said.

"I didn't say he was shot at," Gaze said. "I said he tried to kill 'im. How'd you know he was shot at?"

"Masterson's a gunman," Boswell said. "How else would someone try to kill him? Besides, Harrigan you say? Maddox?"

"We had a hand named Harrigan, Mr. Boswell, but he was fired last week."

"There you go," Boswell said. "No connection to me. What's next?"

"This horse," Clint said. "It came out of your barn."

"Is that a fact? You just took that horse out of my barn?" the rancher asked.

"No," Clint said, "one of your men took it out of the barn last night and led it to a box canyon where the deputy was killed."

"I've got nothing to do with anyone shooting a lawman, Sheriff," Boswell said. "You can't prove otherwise."

"You've got an answer for everything, Mr. Boswell," Bat said, "but as soon as I get a telegram from Amarillo, I'll have some questions you can't answer."

"I'm done with you gentleman," Boswell said. "Get off my land."

"I'm not done with you, Boswell," Gaze said. "I'll have you for the murder of my deputy."

"Good luck."

Clint, Bat and the lawmen exchanged a glance, then turned to leave.

"And if you say that's my horse, I'll thank you to leave it," Boswell said.

Clint looked at him.

"Do you say it's your horse?" Clint asked.

"I had a painted pony, but I don't know if that's the same one, so take it," the rancher said, with a wave of his hand, and went back into the house.

"You heard Mr. Boswell," Maddox said. "Off his land."

"You tell Boswell we'll be back as soon as Tom Corbin implicates him," Bat said.

Then he turned his horse and followed the other men away.

***

Once they got away from the ranch, Bat said, "He had an answer for everything."

"That's what people like that do," Clint said. "They can lie on the spot."

Bat looked at Clint.

"I forgot about your distaste for rich ranchers," the gambler said.

"They all think they can have whatever they want," Clint answered. "Sometimes I think I was put on this earth to see that they don't get it."

"Well," Gaze said, "I'm here to help you make sure that this one doesn't."

"I need a telegram from Amarillo, and a statement from Corbin," Bat said, "and then I think we'll have what we need to move forward."

"I'm thinkin' about Maddox," Greg spoke up.

They all turned and looked at him.

"I always thought he was an honest, decent man," the part-time deputy said. "I wouldn't think he was in line with his boss on this."

"Do you think you could talk to him and convince him to turn?" Bat asked.

"I could give it a try," the young man said. "I'll take Matt with me."

"Good," Gaze said, "do it."

They rode the rest of the way in silence, each alone with their own thoughts on ending this ordeal that started with tons of twisted steel and mangled flesh.

Chapter Thirty-Five

As soon as they arrived in town Bat went to the telegraph office while Clint and Gaze went to the undertaker. The sheriff sent Greg to the office.

"I'm gonna need you to be a little more than a part-time deputy for a while," he told the young man.

"I understand, Sir," Greg said, "Matt, too?"

"Yes," Gaze said. "Let 'im know."

"I will," Greg said. "And I'll talk to Maddox."

"Do that."

Clint and Gaze entered the undertaker's office.

"Sheriff," the man said. "I'm sorry about your deputy. He's in the back. I . . . tried to clean him off."

"Thanks, Ives," Gaze said.

Clint was always surprised how undertakers looked alike. But this one didn't. He looked like a little banker.

"Ives, this is Clint Adams," Gaze said. "Clint, this is Howard Ives."

"Mr. Ives," Clint said, nodding.

"Sir."

"Ives, I want a good coffin, and then just bury him. No fanfare. He didn't have any family in town."

"Yes, sir."

"Thanks."

They left the office and saw Bat coming towards them.

"Did you get a response?" Clint asked.

"Yes, but no help, yet. Reynolds is putting someone on it."

"Who?"

"Heck Thomas."

Gaze was surprised.

"Heck Thomas isn't a railroad detective," he said.

"He's a detective," Bat said, "and friends with William Reynolds."

"Well," Clint said, "he's got two good men working on this, now."

"Don't be modest," Bat said. "We'll all get this cleared up. Let's check on Corbin."

"You do that," Gaze said. "I'm going to my office."

"And I've got something to do," Clint said. "Let's all meet in The Oasis."

They all agreed and went their own ways.

***

Clint went to the hotel to see if Miss Rafferty was in his room. She wasn't. He went to the front desk to see if she had checked into her own room. She had not. Maybe she had gone home. And maybe he was pushing it, and she wasn't involved, at all. She was just from Amarillo. That seemed like too much of a coincidence.

He left the hotel.

***

When the doctor let Bat in, the gambler asked, "How is he?"

"He's awake," the doctor said. "You can have a few minutes."

He took Bat into the exam room. Corbin was lying on his back covered with a sheet and a bandage. He turned his head and looked at Bat.

"You didn't give me a choice," Bat told him. "Why'd you go for your gun?"

"Why do you think?" Corbin asked.

"I know you were involved with Boswell and the railroad wreck," Bat said. "I need to know exactly who you worked for and what you did."

Corbin wet his lips.

"Look, Masterson," he said, "I'm a poker player, just like you—"

"Not like me," Bat said. "Not like me at all."

"Bat," Corbin said, "are you gonna kill me?"

"Tell me what I want to know," Bat said, "and we'll see."

***

Bat joined Clint at The Oasis. He got a beer from the bar and sat down.

"Boswell told Corbin to 'take care' of me," Bat said.

"Did he actually say to kill you?"

"Not in so many words," Bat said, "but he made his needs clear."

"Needs?"

Bat sipped his beer.

"Boswell needs me to stop investigating," he said.

"And?"

"Corbin said Boswell hired him to sabotage the tracks and wreck the train. He didn't tell him what men to use. That was up to him."

"So he's not just a gambler."

"He's whatever somebody wants to pay him to be," Bat said.

"Will he testify against Boswell?"

"He says yes," Bat said, "but we'll have to wait and see."

"This doesn't tell us who killed his deputy," Clint said.

"To save his own ass, Boswell might give us the killer," Bat said.

"Let's talk to the sheriff then."

They both finished their drinks and left the saloon.

Chapter Thirty-Six

Gaze looked up from his desk as they entered.

"Where's Greg?" Clint asked.

"He went back out to the ranch to talk to Maddox."

"He didn't go alone, did he?" Bat asked.

"No," Gaze said, "Matt went with him. They're both wearin' badges."

"That didn't matter with Banner," Clint reminded him.

"He got shot in the back," Gaze said. "They might not have known he was a deputy."

"That's true," Bat said, "but they still killed him."

"What happened with Corbin?" the lawman asked.

"That's why we're here," Bat said.

"Have a seat and tell me."

Clint and Bat sat across from the man, and Bat told him what he had learned from Corbin.

"That sonofabitch!" Gaze hissed. "Sitting in The Oasis playing poker, after wreckin' that train, killin' people—"

"That was his job," Bat said.

"Hired by Boswell?"

"Right."

"And who's behind Boswell?" Gaze asked. "Or workin' with him?"

"That we'll have to get from Boswell," Bat said, "or from something Heck Thomas finds out in Amarillo."

"I could go out there and put him under arrest right now," Gaze said, "but that might not get me Banner's killer. Boswell's got an army of lawyers."

"So we need more," Bat said.

"We need more," Gaze agreed.

"What if we don't need more men, or a lawyer?" Clint asked.

They both looked at him.

"What if we let it be known," Clint said, "that we have enough information to arrest Boswell? What do you think he'd do?"

"Send his lawyers in," Gaze said.

"Or a bunch of killers," Bat said. "Again."

"But this time better ones," Clint said. "Big names, a lot of money."

"And what if they succeed?" Gaze asked. "What if they kill you? Or buy heavy guns?"

"Then you'll get them," Bat said.

"But they're not going to kill us," Clint said, "because we'll be ready."

Gaze sat back in his chair and thought a moment before speaking.

"Let's see what Greg and Matt can get done with Maddox," he said. "Then we can make a plan."

"Okay," Bat said, after looking at Clint. "We'll wait for them to get back."

"So there's nothing to do but wait," Clint said.

Clint looked at Bat and asked, "Poker?"

"Two-handed?"

"Why not?"

They stood and left the office.

***

They played two-handed poker in The Oasis for hours, passing the same money back and forth between them.

"You think we can put this to bed tomorrow?" Clint asked.

"Only if Boswell acts right away, and sends somebody after us," Bat said. "But we can probably do it in the next few days."

"I hope so," Clint said. "I'm kind of tired of this town."

"I don't blame you," Bat said. "I'm especially sorry about Banner. He was so young."

"Yes," Clint said, "he was. So are Greg and Matt."

"We shouldn't have let the sheriff send them out there alone."

"Too late now," Clint said. "Too late."

Chapter Thirty-Seven

When Maddox entered Boswell's office, the man asked, "What's wrong?"

"I just talked to two deputies."

"Where?"

"Not far from here?"

"Why?"

"I know 'em," Maddox said. "They're good boys."

"What did they want?"

"They wanted to warn me I could be in trouble," Maddox said. "They want me to testify."

"Against me?"

"Yes, Sir."

"What did you tell them?"

"I said I would."

"Good," Boswell said. "You did good. Do we have anyone loyal?"

"A couple of men."

"Good. Send them out. I want them back here in the morning with twenty men."

"Yes, sir."

Maddox left the office.

***

Outside, Maddox got Tice and Kitterick together and told them what Boswell wanted.

"Go where?" Tice asked.

"Lubbock," Maddox said. "Mr. Boswell has men there. Go to the Whiskey Time Saloon."

"Got it."

They started to leave, and then Tice stopped and turned.

"Carl, uh, I shot Deputy Banner. I didn't mean to, but I did."

"Yeah, okay. Go!"

Tice and Kitterick ran to the barn to saddle their horses.

***

When Matt and Greg came back to town and entered the sheriff's office, Gaze breathed a sigh of relief.

"Did you see him?" he asked.

"Yes," Greg said, "we got him away from the ranch."

"And?"

"He was nervous," Matt said. "He says he's been loyal to Mr. Boswell, but this thing with the train . . . this went too far."

"So he admits Boswell was behind it?"

"Yes," Greg said.

"And he'll testify to it?"

"Yes."

"Good," Gaze said. "I'll talk to Adams and Masterson, and then we'll go and talk to a judge and get a warrant."

"What about us?"

"You both will be in on the arrest," Gaze promised. "Right now, get some rest."

"Yes, sir."

They left the office together and Gaze headed for The Oasis.

***

When the sheriff joined them, he brought three cold beers to the table.

"Who's winnin'?" he asked.

"Nobody," Bat said.

"Everybody," Clint said.

They put the cards away and took their beers. Gaze told them what Maddox had told the deputies.

"If we get Corbin and Maddox to testify," Bat said, "then we've got him."

"Should we put the word out?" Clint asked.

"Let him know we're comin'?" Gaze asked. "He'll have his killers waitin' for us."

"And he won't be able to plead innocent," Bat said, "or hide behind his lawyers."

"We'll have to kill some people," Gaze said.

"Hired killers," Clint reasoned. "Maybe one of them killed Banner."

"If we take Boswell in, we'll find Ted Banner's killer," Gaze said.

"So you just want to go out and get him," Bat said. "Keep it quiet."

"I'll talk to a judge in the mornin'," Gaze said. "We could decide then."

"We'll come to your office," Clint said. "You can let us know what's happening."

Gaze finished his beer and said, "Right." He rose and left.

Bat looked across the table at Clint.

"Another hand or two?" he asked.

Clint picked up the cards.

"Why not?" he asked.

Chapter Thirty-Eight

In the morning, Sheriff Gaze went to the courthouse to see Judge Cadence.

"Sheriff?" the older man said, as he entered the office.

"I've got a story to tell you, Judge," the lawman said.

"Go ahead and tell it."

***

When the sheriff got back to his office, Clint and Bat were sitting there.

"Did you get a warrant?" Clint asked.

Gaze sat behind his desk, his shoulders slumped.

"He wouldn't give it to me."

"What?" Bat asked.

"He said he needs more," Gaze said, "I'd have to bring him Corbin, Maddox, or both, and they'd have to sign statements."

"Do you think he's working for Boswell?" Bat asked.

"It could be," Gaze said, "but with those statements, he'd have to issue a warrant."

"All right, then," Bat said. "I'll get one from Corbin."

"I'll go out to the ranch with Greg and Matt and get one from Maddox," Gaze said. "Or better yet, bring him to the judge." He looked at Clint. "You wanna come along?"

"I better stay with Bat," Clint said, "just in case."

"Suit yourself." Gaze stood up, and they all left the office together.

***

Clint walked with Bat to the doctor's office.

"You're expecting trouble here," Bat said. "That's why you stayed."

"Can you think of any better backup than each other?" Clint asked. "I don't think Boswell will try to have three more lawmen killed."

"No," Bat said, "just us."

"And we're better off not having anyone else in the way," Clint said.

"Good thinking."

They entered the doctor's office and Bat yelled, "Doc?"

No answer.

"Doc?"

Still no reply.

"Corbin was in here," he said, and opened the door to the examination room.

Corbin wasn't there, and the doctor was on the floor.

"Goddamnit!" Bat roared and leaned over the man.

"Is he dead?" Clint asked.

"No," Bat said. "Help me get him up on the table."

Together they lifted him onto the table and applied a cold cloth to his forehead. His eyelids fluttered open.

"What happened?" he asked.

"You tell us," Bat said. "We found you on the floor, and your patient is gone."

"Somebody hit you on the head," Clint said. "Was it him? Was he able to do that?"

"Probably," the doctor said. "I don't think anyone else was here."

"This is my fault," Bat said. "I should've put a man on him."

"Help me sit up," the doctor said.

"You better lie there a minute and get your bearings," Clint said. "Don't take the blame, Bat. We had no idea he was capable of this."

"We have to find him," Bat said. "I'm thinking he's heading out to Boswell's ranch."

"Isn't everybody?" Clint said.

"The sheriff's already on his way out there," Bat said. "We might as well follow him."

"You going to be okay, Doc?" Clint asked.

"Go," the doctor said, finally sitting up. "I'll be fine."

They left the doctor's office to get their horses.

***

Tice and Kitterick were riding all night to return with the twenty men Boswell demanded. But as they approached the ranch, they spotted a riderless horse up ahead.

"Hold up," Tice said.

The group reined in, and he and Kitterick rode on ahead. As they approached the horse, they saw a man on the ground. Tice dismounted and checked him.

"Is he dead?" Kitterick asked.

"Yeah, he's dead," Tice said, looking up at the man. "It's Corbin. Looks like he was hurt already, but he fell off his horse and landed on his head."

They mounted up again.

"He must've been on his way to the ranch."

"Should we bury him? Or take him along?"

Tice grimaced.

"Yeah, okay," he said, dismounting again, "help me tie him to his horse."

Chapter Thirty-Nine

When the twenty-two men rode onto the ranch, Carl Maddox came out of the house to greet them. He recognized a man named Pete Royal, a gunman he knew Boswell had used before.

"What's that?" he asked, pointing to the man tied to the horse.

"Corbin," Tice said. "We found him along the way."

Maddox walked to the horse to examine the man. He could see he had been shot.

"Who shot 'im?" he asked.

"We don't know," Royal said. "doesn't look like the bullet wound killed him."

"I'm guessing Masterson shot him and he was on his way out here for help," Maddox said. "Mr. Boswell's not gonna like this. Dump his body in the barn for now. Royal, come inside with me."

"The rest of you wait here," Royal said, and followed Maddox into the house.

***

Boswell listened while Maddox told him about Corbin.

"I knew that man was an idiot," he said, when Maddox was finished. "It's just as well he's dead." He looked at the other man. "How many are with you, Royal?"

"Nineteen, sir," Royal replied. "Your men said you wanted twenty."

"That's right," Boswell said. "Have a seat, and a drink." He didn't offer Maddox either of those.

Royal helped himself to a glass of whiskey and sat down.

"That's all, Carl," Boswell said.

"Yes, sir."

"Oh," Boswell said, "bury that idiot somewhere."

"Yes, Sir."

As Maddox left, Boswell asked Royal, "Did my men tell you anything?"

"They said you wanted twenty men," Royal said. "You've got 'em."

This was what Boswell liked about working with Pete Royal. He never asked why.

"You're going up against Clint Adams and Bat Masterson," the rancher said. "Do you have a problem with that?"

"Not for the right amount of money," the man said.

"And your men?"

"They're with me."

"Then this is what I want you to do . . ."

***

"Hold it!" Sheriff Gaze called, putting his hand up and reining in.

"What the hell?" Greg said.

They could see the house from where they were, and all the riders outside.

"They've got a damn army, Sheriff," Matt said. "We're gonna need Mr. Adams and Mr. Masterson."

"And maybe fifty others," Greg said.

"Let's get back to town and figure out what to do," Gaze said.

***

But they didn't have to go all the way back to town. Halfway there they saw Clint and Bat riding toward them.

"What happened at the ranch?" Bat asked.

"We never got there," Gaze said. "Boswell's got an army. I don't know if they're waitin' for us or comin' to get us."

"An army?" Clint asked.

"Well," Gaze said, "at least twenty men with guns. What's bringin' you out here?"

"Corbin knocked out the doctor and ran," Bat said. "We figured he was on his way out here."

"I don't think he made it," Gaze said.

"Why do you say that?" Bat asked.

"We saw a body tied to a horse."

"Yeah," Clint said, "he could've died on the way."

"If Boswell imported the guns, they must be pros," Bat said. "Plus, he's got some of his own."

"Like I said," Gaze commented. "An army. How are we gonna handle this?"

"There's five of us," Clint said. "It wouldn't be smart for us to ride right in. Let's go back to town, wait and see what Boswell's going to do."

"You think he's going all in?" Gaze said. "Sending his army to town?"

"I think he's frustrated, and he's making a huge mistake," Clint said. "He's leaving no doubt in anyone's mind that he was behind the train wreck."

"I don't think the judge is gonna be able to ignore this," Gaze said.

"Then we better get back to town and get ready," Clint said.

"You got a plan?" Bat asked.

"No," Clint said, "but we will by the time we get back to town."

Chapter Forty

They left Matt up the trail to keep an eye out for Boswell's army.

"Don't do anythin' stupid," Gaze said. "Remember Banner."

"I will."

"Just come ridin' in when you see them."

"Yes, Sir."

Clint, Bat, Gaze and Greg rode into town and dismounted.

"You know this town," Bat said to Gaze. "What are the chances we can get some help real quick?"

"Slim to none," Gaze said. "We're on our own."

"We've got Willy and Lester," Bat reminded them, "the conductor and the fireman."

"They're not gunmen," Clint said.

"Me and my deputies aren't either," Gaze said.

"We don't even know if they're still in town," Clint said.

"If they are," Bat said, "we'll just put a gun in their hands. After all, they work for the railroad."

"Well," Clint said, "since you're working for the railroad, you might as well go and find them. Meanwhile, we'll try and figure out a way to welcome Boswell's gunmen."

"Get back here quick," Clint said.

Bat nodded and went off at a run.

***

Pete Royal came out of the ranch house and looked at his men.

"Clint Adams and Bat Masterson are in Dexter," Royal said. "Mr. Boswell is payin' us to get 'em out of Dexter."

"Just the two of 'em?" someone called out.

"And a few lawmen," Royal said, "but our main problems are the Gunsmith and Masterson."

The men exchanged glances and nods.

"This will put Dexter on the map," Pete Royal said, "and, oh yeah, by the way, us, too."

"But are they comin' here or are we goin' there?" another voice asked.

"I don't want to wait," Royal said. "I said we'd go in and get 'em."

The men hesitated.

"The quicker we get it done," Pete Royal said, "the quicker we get paid."

That brought out a roar of approval.

***

When Bat returned to the center of town, he had both Willy and Lester in tow, each armed with a rifle and looking nervous.

"They're both willing," Bat said, "but I don't know if they can hit anything."

"We'll put them each on a rooftop," Clint said. "All they have to do is fire into a crowd. They've got to hit something."

"Good thinking."

Bat looked at the line Clint and the others had drawn across the street, using buckboards.

"I guess this is the best we can do," he said, "assuming they do come into town from that direction."

"If they circle around and come from the other direction, we jump over to the other side," Clint said.

"And if they split their horses and come from both directions?"

"We'll deal with that when the time comes," Clint said. "I'm betting that gunmen hired by Homer Boswell have as big an ego as he has."

"So they'll come right in from there," Bat said, pointing out in the direction of the Boswell ranch.

"That's my bet," Clint said. "The sheriff's, too."

"Where is the sheriff?"

"Trolling the citizenship to see if we can come up with an extra gun or two."

"He didn't hold out much hope for that," Bat reminded him.

"Still doesn't, but what the hell."

"And the deputies?"

"Matt's still out watching the road," Clint said. "Greg went to the sheriff's office to empty his gun rack."

"Good idea," Bat said. "Okay, "I'll get the railroad men placed. Hotel and Saloon rooftops?"

"That's what I figure," Clint said. "Highest vantage points. You wanna get rid of that bowler?"

"Why?"

"It's a big target and you don't want it full of holes."

Bat looked up, then removed the hat and placed it on one of the buckboards.

***

When Sheriff Gaze returned he was alone.

"You know," he said to Clint, "with you and Masterson in town I expected trouble, but I never expected a siege."

"No, I didn't either," Clint said. "I thought Boswell would hide his involvement with an iron hand. I wonder how much his railroad connections are going to like this idea?"

"We ain't heard any more from Heck Thomas yet, huh?" the sheriff asked.

"Not a word."

"You know Thomas?"

"Very well," Clint said. "If there's anything to find out. Heck will find it."

Greg came running up with an armful of rifles.

"Spread 'em out, Greg," Gaze instructed.

"Yes, sir."

There were four buckboards strung across the street. He put a couple of rifles on each.

"You think Boswell's comin' in with them?" Clint asked the sheriff.

"Not a chance," Gaze said. "He's got an ego, but he knows his limitations. He's a businessman, lettin' his money talk for him here."

"Yeah, that's what I figured," Clint said. "He's got to have somebody working with him in Amarillo. Those are definitely businessmen, who aren't going to like this siege. However this comes out, I don't think Homer Boswell is getting his railroad."

"Small favors, at this point."

Chapter Forty-One

Boswell gave Pete Royal some last minute instructions.

"I want them dead," he said.

"I got that," Royal said. "What about the law?"

"Them too, if they get in the way."

"Killin' law's gonna cost extra," the gunman said.

"Don't worry about it," Boswell said. "After you kill them, there won't be anybody left to arrest you. Besides, when it's all over you're getting out of town with your men."

"And my money."

"Of course."

Royal stepped down off the porch and mounted his horse at the head of his already mounted men. Boswell was keeping his cowhands out of the fray, except for Tice and Kitterick.

"Where do you want me, Mr. Boswell?" Maddox asked.

"You stay behind, Maddox," Boswell said. "You can't run my ranch if you're dead."

"Yes, Sir. That suited Maddox just fine. "Uh, how do you think your people at the railroad are gonna feel about this? This isn't exactly business, you know."

"They'll do what I tell them," Boswell said, sticking a cigar in his mouth.

Carl Maddox didn't know what it was like to be that sure of himself about everything.

***

Matt came riding in around midday.

"They're comin' in," he yelled.

"With the sun at their backs," Clint observed.

"Somebody knows what they're doing," Bat observed.

Bat, Clint and Gaze each stood behind a buckboard while the two young deputies shared a space. The two railroad men stood on rooftops, holding their rifles in sweaty shaking hands.

"Hear that?" Clint asked.

The approaching horses sounded like distant thunder, coming closer and closer.

With more men they could have let the gunmen ride into town and then closed a circle around them, but they didn't have nearly enough men for such a maneuver. Clint and Bat knew that their possible success depended mostly on their abilities with a gun. They would not be giving in to the nerves that most of the other combatants in this fray would. Their shots would be precise and well-placed. Clint figured there would be at least a few real pros on the other side, not affected by nerves. But while they had a superior number behind them, they also had that many more bodies to get in their way. All twenty or twenty-five would not be operating with the same efficiency. Clint preferred a smaller number of proficient guns, then a larger number of less efficient ones.

"Don't fire until we do!" Gaze shouted instructions to the two deputies and railroad men.

***

Pete Royal's instructions to his men had been to, "Follow me," and "shoot anything that moves."

"Anythin?" somebody asked.

"I don't care if it's a dog, a woman, a kid or an ant. Shoot it!"

So as the group approached, they all palmed their iron and prepared to fire as soon as they entered town on the main street.

***

Homer Boswell sat behind his desk, leaning back and twirling his cigar between his lips. He imagined he would be able to hear the gunfire all the way from town. And once it was over, he would be virtually assured of entering the high finance world of railroads. The next day he would be on his way to Amarillo to claim his place.

***

Royal led the men to the mouth of town but then, wisely, reined his horse back and made sure that some of his men rode ahead of him.

***

Clint wished he knew who Boswell had hired to head his group of guns. If he and Bat knew him on sight, they would have been able to target him first. Large groups often lost their confidence when they lost their leader.

That was something he had learned many years ago while fighting Indians with the military.

***

Bat Masterson remembered years ago, when he had first started working for the railroad as a detective. He had been involved in sieges like this before, fighting against a large group of men, but few times had there been so many gunmen. Usually they were Chinamen or Irishmen, fighting with clubs or knives.

There was going to be a lot of bloodshed here, over a small, puissant railroad.

After this he was going back to poker, full time.

Chapter Forty-Two

Bat and Gaze had agreed that Clint would fire first. They all held rifles and had extras handy. Once the attacking force got close enough, they would use their pistols. That would be where Clint and Bat could do the most damage, but there would be a lot of reloading necessary. Bat had an extra handgun from the sheriff's office, and Clint had his Colt New Line handy as well.

So Clint watched along his rifle barrel as the riders approached, already firing ineffectively. All they were doing at this point was making noise. He just hoped the others would hold their fire until he pulled his trigger. No point in letting the gunmen know how few guns they really had and where they were until it was necessary.

Clint wondered if Herman Boswell really thought the Gunsmith and Bat Masterson would be foolishly, arrogantly, standing squarely in the middle of the street, waiting for his forces to arrive. Arrogant men usually expected the same behavior from others.

The riders were getting closer. Time to stop thinking, and start shooting.

***

Bat and Clint fired calmly, their first three shots each taking men from their saddles. The three lawmen began to fire right after, with less success. Gaze killed one man, Matt and Greg kept rushing their shots.

Clint turned to them and shouted, “Slow down and aim!”

Clint never aimed. Shooting came as naturally as pointing his finger. But these young deputies *had* to *aim*!

Clint was aware of the two railroad men, one on either side of the street, firing into the crowd of riders. Just by *accident* they had to be hitting *somebody*.

***

Willy and Lester fired their rifles into the crowd as fast as they could. Both men were pleased to see riders knocked from their saddle, while unaware if they had hit any or not.

***

Pete Royal saw his men being knocked from their saddles. There were obviously more men than just Clint Adams and Bat Masterson firing from cover. Royal had expected supposed living legends like them to stand and face trouble. Instead, they had extra guns at their side and were firing from hiding.

Cowards!

He wheeled his horse around and rode the other way as fast as he could.

***

Clint saw the lawman firing with more efficiency now. He was thinking the gunmen would withdraw, regroup and come again, but that didn't seem to be the case. The men were getting in each other's way, falling from their horses, under the hooves of other horses, knocking them off balance and causing them to throw their riders.

When a good number of the gunmen were either lying on the ground or getting to their feet, Clint and Bat stepped out from behind the buckboard and started firing with both hands. When their pistols were empty, they grabbed an extra rifle from a buckboard and walked forward, basically cleaning house.

Suddenly, the shooting stopped and it was quiet.

It was over, almost before it had begun.

***

Clint and Bat walked among the fallen, checking the bodies.

"You know," Bat said, "there was a time when even this kind of work was done with pride."

"People are saying the old West is dead," Clint said, reloading his Colt and holstering it, "they might be right."

Bat turned to each of the railroad men and waved them down, then turned to face the three lawmen.

"Is it over?" Matt asked.

"It's over," Clint said.

"Are they all dead?" Greg asked.

"Some of them turned and ran," Clint said, "the rest are dead. Anybody hurt?"

Sheriff Gaze said, "I got a scratch. That's it."

"We still don't know who their leader was," Bat said.

"If he's not lying here on the ground, maybe he went back to the ranch to report."

"Or," Bat said, "if he turned and ran, he's still running."

Clint turned to Gaze.

"How do you want to play this?"

"I'm goin' to the judge right now for a warrant," he said. "You wanna ride out to get Boswell with me? You and Bat?"

Clint and Bat exchanged a look and then the gambler said, "We wouldn't miss it."

Chapter Forty-Three

Pete Royal didn't run away.

He went back to the ranch to get his money. He figured he had been through enough to get paid.

He burst through the front door and shouted, "Boswell! Where are you?"

When Carl Maddox came out from the rear of the house, the two men faced each other.

"Where's your boss?" Royal demanded.

"Your boss too, remember," Maddox said. "Is the job done?"

"You bet it's done," Royal said. "The Gunsmith and Masterson came out on top, and I want my money."

"Why is that?" Boswell asked, coming from the back. "If you lost, you don't get paid. And I'll find somebody else to do the job."

"That ain't the way I see it."

"Well, that's the way it is," Boswell said. "Throw this man out, Maddox."

The foreman knew he wasn't a gunman.

"Mr. Boswell—" he started, but he didn't get any further. Royal drew and fired, hitting Maddox in the forehead. He was dead before he hit the ground.

"Now pay me," Royal said, still holding his gun.

Boswell looked down at his dead foreman, then said, "Very well, follow me."

He led the gunman to his office and went around behind his desk quickly—too quickly for Royal.

"Stop!"

Boswell froze.

"Move away from the desk," Royal said, gesturing with the gun.

Boswell did as he was told. Royal walked to the desk and opened a couple of drawers. He found the gun Boswell was going for.

"Not smart," the gunman said, sticking the gun in his belt. "Where's your money?"

"In my safe," Boswell said, pointing to the safe in the corner.

"Open it."

Boswell walked to the safe and knelt on one knee in front of it.

"You know," he said, while dialing the combination, "you won't be getting any more work from me after this."

"That's okay," Royal said, "I expect there to be enough money in the safe to make up for it."

Boswell looked over his shoulder.

"You're going to take it all?"

"Every penny."

"Royal—"

"Open it!"

Boswell finished dialing and opened the door.

"Take it out, all of it."

Boswell took stacks of bills from the safe, and then some papers.

"What's that?" Royal asked.

"Just some papers," Boswell said, putting them on the desk.

"Move away."

The older man stepped back.

Royal went to the desk, picked up the stacks of bills, and to Boswell's relief, left the papers.

"Don't leave this room for half an hour," the gunman told Boswell.

"I won't."

Royal started for the door, then stopped as something occurred to him.

"You wouldn't be thinkin' about sending someone after me, would you?"

"Of course not," Boswell said, "what good would that do?"

Royal turned and pointed his gun at Boswell.

"I could just kill you and make sure."

"Now wait—"

***

Clint and Bat rode to the Boswell ranch while Gaze saw the judge. They thought it made more sense that way, just in case somebody was riding there to tell him what happened.

As they rode onto the ranch, it looked deserted. The hands had either left or were out on the range. On the porch they could see a body.

They dismounted and turned the body over. It was the foreman, shot in the forehead.

"What the hell—" Clint started, but at that moment there was a shot from inside the house.

"Want to go in?" Bat asked.

"Let's wait and see who comes out."

They got off the porch and stood by their horses. Minutes later, the front door opened, and a man stepped out. He was tall, rangy, in his forties, and looked like he had something stuffed in his shirt.

"You should've kept your gun in your hand, Pete," Clint said.

"You know this fella?" Bat asked.

"Pete Royal," Clint said, "cheap gun-for-hire."

"Cheap" Royal asked. "Are you Masterson?"

"I am," Bat said. "William Barclay Masterson, at your service."

"What's in your shirt, Pete?"

"Money," Royal said. "Enough for the three of us."

"And Boswell?"

"He won't be a problem."

"That how you wind up most of your business dealings?" Bat asked.

"He didn't tell me you'd have help, and you'd be hidin'," Royal said.

"Hiding?" Clint said, laughing. "You had twenty men with you."

"Are they dead?" Royal asked.

"Seventeen of them are," Clint said. "The rest ran off, like you."

"I didn't run. I came here to get paid." He touched the bundle in his shirt. "I did. Now I'm leavin'. Unless one of you want to stop me."

"We both do," Clint said. "It's just a matter of who."

Royal hesitated, then asked, "What if I left you the money. Would you let me go?"

"Not a chance," Bat said.

"Okay, then," Royal said, shaking out his arms and spreading his feet, "which one?"

Chapter Forty-Four

Clint and Bat stepped over Royal's body, took a moment to look inside his shirt. There was money there, covered with blood from Clint's bullet.

They entered the house and found their way to Boswell's office. He was seated behind his desk, with a bullet through the heart.

"What the hell—" they heard Sheriff Gaze, coming down the hall. He entered the room on the run. "What happened?"

"That's Pete Royal out there," Clint said. "A gunman. He killed Maddox and Boswell and cleaned out the safe. I killed him."

"So now what?" Gaze asked. "Who do I arrest?"

"Somebody from the railroad must've been working with Boswell." Bat said. "Let's see if there's anything here to tell us who."

"You two look," Gaze said, "I've got Matt and Greg outside. We'll collect the bodies."

Gaze left the room and Clint and Bat started searching. It didn't take long. Clint looked in the safe, but Bat looked on top of the desk.

"Here we go," he said, picking up some papers.

"What's that?"

"Signed papers between Boswell and one of the board members of the railroad."

"Do you know the board member?"

"No," Bat said, "but I will. I'm going to Amarillo."

"When?"

"Tomorrow," Bat said. "Care to take a ride?"

Clint looked around the messy room, and said, "I don't see why not?"

***

They helped the lawmen get Boswell's body outside and onto a buckboard with the others.

As Matt and Greg drove off in the buckboard with their horses tied to the back, Gaze turned to Bat and Clint.

"What's next?" he asked.

"You've full-filled your warrant," Clint said. "You've got Boswell."

"I guess so. What's next for you two?"

"I'm taking Clint to Amarillo with me," Bat said. "We'll take the guilty man there in custody, which will fulfill my obligation to William Reynolds and his railroad."

"Coming back?" Gaze said.

"Never," Bat said.

"Likewise," Clint said.

"But we'll ride back with you now," Bat added.

"What should we do with the money that was inside the man's shirt?"

"I don't know," Bat said. "It might belong to the railroad. Put it in the bank until somebody figures it out."

"That'll be up to somebody else."

They mounted up and rode back to town.

***

The next morning Gaze met Clint and Bat outside the livery stable as they walked their horses out.

"Thought I'd see you off," he said.

"That's good of you," Bat said.

"If you like," Clint said, "we can send you a telegram and tell you how it turned out."

"Maybe even tell you what to do with the money," Bat added.

"That suits me."

The three men shook hands, then Clint and Bat mounted up and rode out.

Chapter Forty-Five

Amarillo was an easy ride. Clint and Bat registered at a fairly posh hotel, Bat assuring Clint his room would be covered. When they met in the lobby to have a meal together, Bat was replete with a new suit, a bowler, and a walking stick with a gold knob.

"You're beautiful," Clint said. "All I did was take a bath."

"And I appreciate it," Bat said. "We can eat here."

"When do we see your friend, Reynolds?"

"We'll call on him in the morning."

"What's on the agenda for tonight?" Clint asked, as they walked to the dining room.

"After dinner? Some drinking, some poker, a good night's sleep. You're welcome to join me. Oh, except for the good night's sleep, of course."

They sat and ordered steaks.

After they ate, the night went as planned, and then they each went to their own room for that good night's sleep.

***

In the morning they had breakfast in the same place, then went out front and flagged a horse drawn cab to the building where William Reynolds had his office.

"Is this the office of the railroad?" Clint asked as they got out of the cab.

"It's his office," Bat said. "The railroad is just one of his businesses."

They entered the building and went up to the second floor. As they entered the office with WILLIAM REYNOLDS written on it, a middle-aged woman looked up at them.

"William Barclay Masterson and Clint Adams to see Mr. Reynolds," Bat said.

"Yes, sir," she said. "One moment."

"She stood up and went through a connecting door. Moments later she opened it, stepped out and said, "You may go right in."

"Thank you," Bat said, and he and Clint entered.

A tall, gaunt looking man in his sixties stood behind his desk and extended his hand.

"Bat," he said, "can't tell you how glad I am to see you."

"Bill, this is Clint Adams. He was a big help."

"Yes, Mr. Adams," Reynolds said, shaking his hand, "I'm glad you came along when you did. Have a seat, both of you."

They all sat.

"What've you got for me?" Reynolds asked.

Bat leaned forward and passed over the papers he had found on Boswell's desk. Reynolds took the time to read them thoroughly.

"Sonsofbitches!" Reynolds seethed.

"Did you trust both those men?" Bat asked.

"I don't trust anyone I do business with."

"That's a hard way to do business," Clint said.

"I'm sure that's the way you live your whole life, Mr. Adams," Reynolds said.

"Touché," Clint said.

Reynolds put the paperwork down on his desk.

"I'll have them picked up," he said. "I'd like you to be there, Bat."

"Sure."

"Mind if I tag along?" Clint asked.

"Not at all," Reynolds said. "I'll have you both picked up at your hotel this afternoon. We'll get it over with."

"We'll be waiting," Bat said.

They stood and started from the office. Clint stopped at the door and turned back.

"I have a question, Mr. Reynolds," he said.

"What's that?"

"Miss Rafferty," he said. "Was she working for you?"

"Rafferty?" Reynolds frowned. "Oh, the teacher. No, she wasn't. Why?"

"Just curious," Clint said, and walked out.

***

Outside the building they flagged another cab.

"Where to, gents?" the driver asked.

They told him to take them to their hotel.

"What was that about the teacher?" Bat asked, along the way.

"Just curious," Clint said.

When they reached the hotel, they got down and entered. To their left was the dining room, and to the right the hotel bar.

"A drink?" Bat asked.

"Why not?"

They entered the saloon, got two beers and claimed a back table. The place was almost empty, and the businessmen who were there paid them no attention.

"Reynolds seemed annoyed," Clint said, "but not surprised."

"Like he said," Bat replied, "he doesn't trust anyone he does business with."

Bat took a sip and then took out a deck of cards.

"Two-handed?" he asked.

"Why not?"

Chapter Forty-Six

When the police detectives came into the bar, Clint and Bat had been sending the same bills back and forth across the table for hours.

"Mr. Masterson? Mr. Adams?" one of them said.

"That's right."

"I'm Lieutenant Caine, this is Sergeant Oswald. We were told to pick you up and take you with us."

Clint and Bat stood up.

"Let's go," Bat said.

***

The first man's name on the papers with Homer Boswell was a businessman, Andrew Palmer. They picked him up at his office.

"This is a mistake," he complained.

"Don't bother," Bat said, "we have the signed papers."

Palmer's shoulders slumped.

***

The second man was a banker, Franklin L. Dalby. When he saw the four men enter his club, he abandoned his lunch and put his hands up.

Both men were taken to jail, where William Reynolds signed the complaint. He, Bat and Clint left the police station.

"Thank you both," he said, shaking hands with them both.

"What are friends for, Bill?" Bat asked.

As Reynolds walked away and got into his carriage, Clint looked at Bat and asked, "Where are you off to?"

"I'll send that telegram to Sheriff Gaze in Dexter, and then get back to my life. But first I'm buying my friend Heck Thomas dinner. Want to join us?"

"Be happy to, but first I've got something to do."

"What's that?"

With a smile Clint said, "I'm off to school."

Upcoming New Release

THE GUNSMITH
J.R. ROBERTS

40TH ANNIVERSARY EDITION

THE FRIENDLY MINE
BOOK 480

Clint Adams comes to Denver at the invitation of his friend, Talbot Roper. The best private detective in the country is about to embark on a new venture. He owns part of a new gold mine in Nelson, Nevada. He wants Clint not only to be his partner, but to look the mine over and advise him on whether or not it's a good investment. When they arrive, they discover that others are also interested in the mine. While they are investigating the mine's potential, they are also fighting to keep it. In this 40th anniversary edition of the Gunsmith series, will Clint Adams strike it rich?

For more information
visit: www.SpeakingVolumes.us

Upcoming New Release

THE GUNSMITH GIANT
J.R. ROBERTS

SPECIAL THANKSGIVING EDITION

THE GUNSMITH TURKEY SHOOT

Trying to decide whether he should spend Thanksgiving alone on the trail or accept one of several invitations from friends to spend it with their family. Clint Adams rides into the town of Belle Fourche, South Dakota and finds himself roped into officiating a turkey shoot competition. Seemingly a simple task, Clint soon finds that he's been sucked into a situation that is anything but simple. Thanksgiving suddenly turns into a deadly holiday that must be survived, not celebrated.

On Sale!

THE GUNSMITH GIANT SERIES

For more information

visit: www.SpeakingVolumes.us

On Sale!

LADY GUNSMITH
BOOKS 1 - 10

For more information
visit: www.SpeakingVolumes.us

On Sale!

AWARD-WINNING AUTHOR
ROBERT J. RANDISI (J.R. ROBERTS)

For more Information
visit: www.SpeakingVolumes.us

On Sale!

TALBOT ROPER NOVELS
ROBERT J. RANDISI

For more information
visit: www.SpeakingVolumes.us